Joaquin Miller

Songs of Italy

Joaquin Miller

Songs of Italy

ISBN/EAN: 9783744770538

Printed in Europe, USA, Canada, Australia, Japan

Cover: Foto ©Andreas Hilbeck / pixelio.de

More available books at **www.hansebooks.com**

Songs of Italy.

BY

JOAQUIN MILLER,

AUTHOR OF "SONGS OF THE SIERRAS," ETC.

BOSTON:
ROBERTS BROTHERS.
1878.

TO

HENRY WADSWORTH LONGFELLOW.

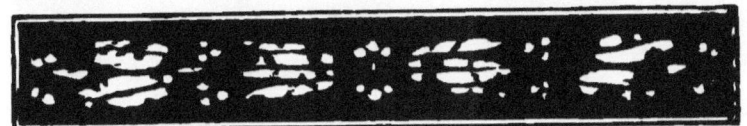

CONTENTS.

ROME 11

A DOVE OF ST. MARK 13

SUNRISE IN VENICE 29

PALATINE HILL 32

IN A GONDOLA 34

COMO 36

A GARIBALDIAN'S STORY 42

THE IDEAL AND THE REAL 50

THE IDEAL AND THE REAL, PART II. 68

IL CAPUCIN 75

FAITH 79

TO FLORENCE 81

FOR PAULINE 83

TO CARRIE A. S. 85

THE UNKNOWN TONGUE 87

UNICA-ÆTERNA 89

Sirocco 92
Pace Implora 94
Alone 97
Implora 99
The Quest of Love 100
O Love 102
After the Boar-Hunt 104
Dolce far niente 107
To the Lion of St. Mark 109
To the Lion of St. Mark again 111
Under the Lion of St. Mark at Night . . 113
To Santa Barbara of Venice 115
A Storm in Venice 117
A Hail-Storm in Venice 119
Farewell to the Lion of St. Mark . . . 121
After all 124
Maime mia 127
The Winged Lion once more 128
Cavalier vs. Cavalier 131
A Prince of Rome 133
Gambler or Prince 138
A Peasant's Plea 140
A Dream of Venice 142
For the Nile 144
Vespers in San Marco 146
Recollection 147

CONTENTS.

TORCELLO 150

ATTILA'S THRONE : TORCELLO 151

SANTA MARIA : TORCELLO 158

LILIAN 162

LIFE 164

IN PÈRE LA CHAISE 165

LONGING FOR HOME 168

PESTAM 170

TITIAN'S LAND 171

IN INNSBRUCK 173

FOR PRINCESS MAUD 174

I SHALL REMEMBER 176

VALE 178

SONGS OF ITALY.

ROME.

I.

OME levelled hills, a wall, a dome
That lords its gilded arch and
lies,
While at its base a beggar cries
For bread, and dies, — and that is
Rome.

II.

Yet Rome is Rome; and Rome she must
And shall remain beside her gates,
And tribute take of kings and States,
Until the stars have fallen to dust.

III.

Yea, Time on yon campagnian plain
Has pitched in siege his battle tents;
And round about her battlements
Has marched and trumpeted in vain.

IV.

These skies are Rome! The very loam
Lifts up and speaks in Roman pride;
And Time, outfaced and still defied,
Sits by and wags his beard at Rome,

ROME, 1873.

A DOVE OF SAINT MARK.

I.

THE high-born beautiful snow came down,
  Silent and soft as the terrible feet
Of Time on the mosses of ruins. Sweet
Was the Christmas time in the watery town.
'Twas a kind of carnival swelled the sea
Of Venice that night, and canal and quay
Were alive with humanity. Man and maid,
Glad in their revel and masquerade,
Moved through the feathery snow in the night,
And shook black locks as they laughed out-
    right.

II.

From Santa Maggiore, and to and fro,
And ugly and black as if devils cast out,
Black streaks through the night in the soft, white
    snow,
The steel-prowed gondolas paddled about:
There was only the sound of the long oars' dip,
As the low moon sailed up the sea like a ship
In a misty morn.   Then the low moon rose,
Veiled and vast, through the feathery snows —
And a poet sat pensive and still in his boat,
His mantle held tight in his hand to his throat.

III.

The dreamer arose as he drew to the land,
Threw back his cloak, stood tall and grand,
Then snapped his fingers right sharp as he leapt
To the shore and turned from the quay, and kept
His white brow wrinkled.   He talked aloud
To himself as he melted away with the crowd,
And the feathery snows blew out of the town.
Like a signal light through the night let down
A far star fell through the dim profound,
As a jewel that slipped God's hand to the ground.

IV.

"On the gray, smooth base of your columned
  stone,
Grim old lion of grand St. Mark,
I shall sit me down in your salt-flood town,
While you sit lorded on your granite throne:
Down under your wings on the edge of the sea
In the dim of the lamps, on the rim of the dark,
Alone and in crowds I shall sit me down.
O King on your column, so sullenly,
Wrinkle your brows and tumble your mane!
But the bride comes not to her spouse again.

V.

"Heavens! how beautiful!   Up and down,
Alone and in couples, they glide and they pass,
Silent and dreamy, as if seen in a glass,
And masked to the eyes, in their Adrian town.
Such women!   It breaks one's heart to think.
Water! and never a drop to drink!
What types of Titian!   What glory of hair!
How tall as the sisters of Saul!   How fair!
Sweet flowers of flesh all blossoming,
As if 'twere Eden and Eden's spring.

VI.

"They are talking aloud with all their eyes,
Yet passing me by with never one word.
O pouting sweet lips, do you know there are lies
That are told with the eyes, and never once
    heard
Above a heart's beat when the soul is stirred?
It is time to fly home, O doves of St. Mark!
Take boughs of the olive; bear these to your ark,
And rest and be glad, for the seas and the skies
Of Venice are fair. . . . What! never a home?
What! stained and despised as the soiled sea-
    foam?

VII.

"And who then are you? You look so fair!
Your sweet child-face, as a rose half-blown,
From under your black and abundant hair? . . .
A child of the street, and unloved and alone!
Unloved and alone? . . . There is something then
Between us two that is not unlike! . . .
The strength and the purposes of men
Fall broken idols. We aim and strike
With high-born zeal and with proud intent,
Yet all things turn on an accident.

VIII.

" Nay, I'll not preach. Time's lessons pass
Like twilight's swallows. They chirp in their
  flight,
And who takes heed of the wasting glass?
Night follows day, and day follows night,
And no thing rises on earth but to fall
Like leaves, with their lessons most sad and fit.
They are spread like a volume each year to all :
Yet men nor women learn aught of it,
Or after it all, but a weariness
Of soul and body, and untold distress.

IX.

" Yea, sit, sweet child, by my side, and we —
We will talk of the world. Nay, let my hand
Run round your waist, and, so, let your face
Fall down on my shoulder, and you shall be
My dream of sweet Italy. Here in this place,
Alone in the crowds of this old careless land,
I will mantle your form till the morn, and
  then —
Why, I shall return to the world and to men,
And no whit stained for the one kind word
Which only you and the night may have heard.

X.

"Fear nothing for me, for I shall not fear.
The day, my darling, comes after the night.
The nights they were made to show the light
Of the stars in heaven, tho' storms are near......
Do you see that figure of Fortune up there,
That tops the Dogana with toe a-tip
Of the great gold ball? Her scroll is a-trip
To the turning winds. She is light as the air.
Well, trust to Fortune. Bread on the wave
Turns ever ashore to the hand that gave.

XI.

"What am I? who am I? and what would
    I choose?
Why, I am a poet—a lover of all
That is lovely to see.... Nay, naught shall befall,
For I would not choose what you should refuse.
Yes, I am a failure. I plot and plan,
Give splendid advice to my fellow-man,
Yet ever fall short of achievement.... Ah me!
In my life's early, sad afternoon,
Say, what have I left but a love, or a rune,
A hand reached out to a soul at sea,
Or fair, forbidden, sweet fruit to choose,
That 'twere sin to touch, and—sin to refuse?

XII.

" What! I to go home with you, girl, to-night?
To nestle you down and to call you love?
Well, that were a fancy!   To feed a dove,
A poor, soiled dove of this dear Saint Mark,
Too frightened for rest and too weary for flight.
Nay, nay, my sister; in spite of you,
Sister and tempter, I will be true.
Lo! here by the lion, alone in the dark,
Side by side we two will sit here,
Breathing the beauty as an atmosphere.

XIII.

" We will talk of your poets, of their tales of
    love.
What! cannot read?   Why you never heard then
Of your Desdemona, nor the daring men
Who died for passion?   My poor white dove!
There's a story of Shylock that would drive you
    wild. —
You never have heard of your poets, my child?
Of Tasso, of Petrarch? Not the Bridge of Sighs?
Nor the tale of Ferrara? Nor the thousand whys
That your Venice was ever adored above
All other fair lands for her songs of love?

XIV.

"What then about Shylock?   'Twas gold —
    yes — dead.
The lady?   'Twas love.   Why, yes; she too
Is dead.   And Byron?   'Twas fame — ah, true.
Tasso and Petrarch?   They perished the same.
Yes, so endeth all, as you well have said.
And you, poor child, are too wise, and you,
Too sudden, sad child, in your hard ugly youth,
Have stumbled face fronting an obstinate truth.
For whether for love, for gold, or for fame,
They but lived their day, and they died the
    same.

XV.

"But talk not of death: of death, or the life
That comes after death.   'Tis beyond your reach,
And this too much thought has a sense of
    strife . . .
Ay, true; I promised you not to preach . . .
My maid of Venice, or maid unmade,
Lie still on my bosom.   Be not afraid.
What!   Say you are hungry?   Well, let us dine
Till the near morn comes on the silver shine
Of the lamp-lit sea.   At dawn of day,
Child of the street, you can go your way.

XVI.

Your mother's palace? I know your town ;
Know every nook of it, left and right,
As well as yourself.   For up and down
Your salt-flood streets, for many a night,
I have rowed and roved with a lady fair
As the face of heaven.   Nay, I know there
Is no such a palace.   What ! you dare
To look in my face, to lie outright,
To bend your brows, and to frown me down ?
There is no such a place in that part of the town !

XVII.

" What ! woo me away to your rickety boat,
To pick my pockets, to cut my throat,
With help of your pirates ?   Then throw me out,
Loaded with stones to sink me down,
Down into the filth and dregs of the town ?
Why, that is your damnable aim, no doubt !
And, beautiful child, you seem too fair,
Too young, for even a thought like that ;
Too young for even the soul to dare —
Ay, even the serpent to whisper at.

XVIII.

" Now, there is such a thing as being true
Even in villany. Listen to me :
Black-skinned women and low-browed men,
And desperate robbers and thieves ; and then,
Why, there are the pirates! Ay, pirates re-
    formed,
Pirates reformed and unreformed :
Pirates for me, friends for you. —
And these are your neighbors. And so you see
That I know your town, your neighbors: and I —
Well, pardon me, girl, — but I know you lie.

XIX.

" Tut, tut, my beauty ! What trickery now ?
Why, tears through your hair on my hand like
    rain !
Come ! look in my face : laugh, lie again
With your wonderful eyes. Lift up your brow.
Come ! shake your fist at the world, and defy
The world. Now, this lying is no new thing —
The wearers of laces know well how to lie ;
As well, ay, better, than you or I. . . .
They lie for fortune, for fame : instead,
You, child of the street, only lie for your bread.

. . . .

XX.

" Some sounds blow in from the distant land ;
The bells strike sharp, and as out of tune,
Some sudden, short notes.   To the east and afar,
And up from the sea, is lifting a star
As large, my beautiful child, and as white
And as lovely to see as your little white hand.
The people have melted away with the night,
And not one gondola frets the lagoon.
See !   Away to the east — 'tis the face of morn.
Hear !   Away to the west — 'tis the fisherman's
    horn.

XXI.

" 'Tis morn in Venice !   My child, adieu !
Arise, poor beauty, and go your way ;
And as for myself, why, much like you,
I must sell this story to who may pay
And dares to reckon it brave and meet.
Yea, each of us traders, poor child of pain ;
For each must barter for bread to eat
In a world of trade and an age of gain ;
With just this difference, child of the street :
You sell your body, I sell my brain.

XXII.

" Why, child, what a wreck!   Lo, here you reel,
Poor, wrecked little vessel, with never a keel ;
With never a soul to advise or to care :
You lie like a sea-weed, well astrand,
Blown like the sea-foam hard on the sand,
A poor, white body, with never a hand
Reached out from the land, though you sink and
    die, —
All covered with sin to the brows and hair,
Left all alone to starve or to lie,
Or to sell your body to who may buy.

XXIII.

" Child of the street, I will kiss you !   Yea,
I will fold you and hold you close to my breast.
And as you lie resting in your first rest,
And as night is pushed back from the face of day,
I will push your tumbled and long, strong hair
Well back from your face, and kiss you where
Your ruffian, bearded, black men of crime
Have stung you and stained you a thousand
    time ;
And call you my sister, sweet child, as you sleep,
And waken you not, lest you wake but to weep.

XXIV.

" Yea, tenderly kiss you. And I shall not be
Ashamed, nor stained in the least, sweet dove, —
Tenderly kiss, with the kiss of Love,
And of Faith and of Hope and of Charity.
Nay, I shall be purer and better then ;
For, child of the street, you, living or dead,
Stained to the brows, are purer to me
Ten thousand times than the world of men,
Who but reach you a hand to lead you astray. —
But the dawn is upon us ! Rise, go your way.

XXV.

" Here ! take this money. Take it, and say,
When you have awakened and I am away,
Roving the world and forgetting of you ;
When you have aroused from your brief little rest,
And find these francs nestled down in your
      breast,
And rough men question you, — why, then say
That Madonna sent them. Then kneel and pray,
And pray for me, the worst of the two :
Then God will bless you, sweet child, and you
Shall be mine angel my whole life through.

XXVI.

" Take this money and buy you bread,
And eat and rest while a year wears through.
Then, rising refreshed, try virtue instead ;
Be stronger and better, poor, pitiful dear,
So prompt with a falsehood, prompt with a tear,
For the hand grows stronger as the heart grows
    true.
Take courage, my child, for I promise you
We are judged by our chances of life and lot,
And your poor little soul may yet pass through
The eye of the needle, where laces shall not.

XXVII.

" Poor dove of the dust, with tear-wet wings,
Homeless and lone as the dove from its ark, —
Do you reckon yon angel that tops St. Mark,
That tops the tower, that tops the town,
If he knew us two, if he knew all things,
Would say, poor child, you are worse than I ?
Do you reckon yon angel, looking down
And down like a star, he hangs so high,
Could tell which one were the worst of us two?
Child of the street — it is not you !

XXVIII.

" If we two were dead, and laid side by side
Right here on the pavement, this very day,
Here under the lion and over the sea,
Where the morn flows in like a rosy tide,
And the sweet Madonna that stands in the moon,
With her crown of stars, just across the lagoon,
Should come and should look upon you and me, —
Do you reckon, my child, that she would decide,
As men do decide and as women do say,
That you are so dreadful, and turn away?

XXIX.

" If the angel were sent to choose to-day
Between us two as we lay here,
Dead and alone in this desolate place, —
You, white with a hunger and stained with a tear,
Or I, the rover the whole world through,
Restless and stormy as any sea, —
If the angel were sent to choose, I say,
This very moment the best of the two,
Looking us two right straight in the face,
Child of the street, he would not choose me.

XXX.

" The fresh sun is falling on turret and tower,
The far sun is flashing on spire and dome,
The marbles of Venice are bursting to flower,
The marbles of Venice are flower and foam :
Child of the street, oh, waken you now !
There ! bear my kiss on your brave white brow,
Through earth to heaven : and when we meet
Beyond the waters, poor waif of the street,
Why, then I shall know you, my sad, sweet dove,
And claim you and kiss you with the kiss of love.

VENICE, 1873.

SUNRISE IN VENICE.

I.

NIGHT seems troubled and scarce asleep;
　　Her brows are gathered in broken rest.
A star in the east starts up from the deep!
Sullen old lion of loved Saint Mark,
Lord of the deep, high-throned in the dark!
'Tis morn, new-born, with a star on her breast,
White as my lilies that grow in the West!

Hist! men are passing me hurriedly.
I see the yellow wide wings of a bark!
Sail silently over my morning-star,
And on and in to an amber sea.
I see men move in the moving dark,
Tall and silent as columns are,
Girded and patient as Destiny;
Great, sinewy men that are good to see,
With hair pushed back, and with open breasts;
Barefooted fishermen, seeking their boats,
Brown as walnuts and hairy as goats, —
Brave old water-dogs, wed to the sea,
First to their labors and last to their rests.

II.

Ships are moving! I hear a horn —
A silver trumpet it sounds to me,
Deep-voiced and musical, far at sea . . .
Answers back, and again it calls.
'Tis the sentinel boats that watch the town
All night, as mounting her watery walls,
And watching·for pirate or smuggler.   Down
Over the sea, and reaching away,
And against the east, a soft light falls
Silvery soft as the mist of morn,
And I catch a breath like the breath of day.

III.

The east is blossoming! Yea, a rose,
Vast as the heavens, soft as a kiss,
Sweet as the presence of woman is,
Rises and reaches, and widens and grows
Large and luminous up from the sea,
And out of the sea, as a blossoming tree.

Richer and richer, so higher and higher,
Deeper and deeper it takes its hue;

Brighter and brighter it reaches through
The space of heaven and the place of stars,
Till all is as rich as a rose can be,
And my rose-leaves fall into billows of fire.
Then beams reach upward as arms from a sea;
Then lances and arrows are aimed at me.
Then lances and spangles and spars and bars
Are broken and shivered and strown on the sea;
And around and about me tower and spire
Start from the billows like tongues of fire.

VENICE, 1874.

PALATINE HILL.

I.

A WOLF–LIKE stream without a sound
Steals by and hides beneath the shore,
Its awful secrets evermore
Within its sullen bosom bound.

II.

And this was Rome, that shrieked for room
To stretch her limbs ! A hill of caves
For half-wild beasts and hairy slaves;
And gypsies tent within her tomb!

III.

Two lone palms on the Palatine,
Two rows of cypress black and tall,
With white roots set in Cæsar's Hall, —
A garden, convent, and sweet shrine.

IV.

Tall cedars on a broken wall,
That look away toward Lebanon,
And seem to mourn for grandeur gone:
A wolf, an owl, — and that is all.

Rome, September, 1873.

3

IN A GONDOLA.

I.

'TWAS night in Venice.   Then down to the
        tide,
Where a tall and a shadowy gondolier
Leaned on his oar, like a lifted spear : —
'Twas night in Venice; then side by side
We sat in his boat.   Then oar a-trip
On the black boat's keel, then dip and dip ; —
These boatmen should build their boats more
        wide,
For we were together, and side by side.

II.

The sea it was level as seas of light,
As still as the light ere a hand was laid
To the making of lands, or the seas were made.
'Twas fond as a bride on her bridal night
When a great love swells in her soul like a sea,
And makes her but less than divinity.
'Twas night, — The soul of the day, I wis :
A woman's face hiding from her first kiss.

III.

'Twas night in Venice. On o'er the tide —
These boats they are narrow as they can be,
These crafts they are narrow enough, and we,
To balance the boat, sat side by side —
Out under the arch of the Bridge of Sighs,
On under the arch of the star-sown skies:
We two were together on the Adrian Sea, —
The one fair woman of the world to me.

IV.

These narrow-built boats, they rock when at sea,
And they make one afraid. So she leaned to me;
And that is the reason alone there fell
Such golden folds of abundant hair
Down over my shoulder, as we sat there.
These boatmen should build their boats more
    wide,
Wider for lovers; as wide — Ah, well!
But who is the rascal to kiss, and tell?

VENICE, 1874.

COMO.

THE red-clad fishers row and creep
   Below the crags, as half asleep,
Nor ever make a single sound.
    The walls are steep,
    The waves are deep;
And if a dead man should be found
By these same fishers in their round,
Why, who shall say but he was drowned?

I.

The lakes lay bright as bits of broken moon
Just newly set within the cloven earth;
The ripened fields drew round a golden girth
Far up the steeps, and glittered in the noon;
And, when the sun fell down, from leafy shore
Fond lovers stole in pairs to ply the oar.
The stars, as large as lilies, flecked the blue;
From out the Alps the moon came wheeling
    through
The rocky pass the great Napoleon knew.

II.

A gala night it was, — the season's prime.
We rode from castled lake to festal town,
To fair Milan — my friend and I ; rode down
By night, where grasses waved in rippled
    rhyme :
And so, what theme but love at such a time ?
His proud lip curled the while with silent scorn
At thought of love ; and then, as one forlorn,
He sighed ; then bared his temples, dashed with
    gray ;
Then mocked, as one outworn and well *blasé.*

III.

A gorgeous tiger lily, flaming red, —
So full of battle, of the trumpet's blare,
Of old-time passion, — upreared its head.
I galloped past.   I leaned, I clutched it there
From out the long, strong grass.   I held it high,
And cried : " Lo ! this to-night shall deck her hair
Through all the dance.   And mark ! the man
    shall die
Who dares assault, for good or ill design,
The citadel where I shall set this sign."

IV.

He spake no spare word all the after while.
That scornful, cold, contemptuous smile of his!
And in the hall the same old, hateful smile!
Why, better men have died for less insult than
    this.
Then marvel not that when she graced the floor,
With all the beauties gathered from the four
Far quarters of the world, and she, my fair,
The fairest, wore within her midnight hair
My tiger lily, — marvel not, I say,
That he glared like some wild beast well at bay.

V.

Oh, she shone fairer than the summer star,
Or curled, sweet moon in middle destiny;
More fair than sunrise climbing up the sea,
Where all the loves of Adriana are.
Who loves, who truly loves, will stand aloof:
The noisy tongue makes most unholy proof
Of shallow passion. . . . All the while afar
From out the dance I stood and watched my
    star,
My tiger lily borne an oriflamme of war.

VI.

Italia's beauties blushed at love's advance.
Like bright white mice in moonlight at their
　　play,
Or sunfish shooting in some shining bay,
The swift feet shot and glittered in the dance.
Oh, have you loved and truly loved, and seen
Aught else the while than your own stately
　　queen?
Her presence it was majesty — so tall;
Her proud development encompassed all.
She filled all space.　I sought, I saw but her:
I followed as some fervid worshipper.

VII.

Adown the dance she moved with matchless
　　grace.
The world — my world — moved with her.
　　Suddenly
I questioned whom her cavalier might be?
'Twas he !　His face was leaning to her face !
I clutched my blade ;　I sprang ;　I caught my
　　breath, —
And so, stood leaning cold and still as death.

And they stood still. She blushed, then reached
 and tore
The lily as she passed, and down the floor
She strewed its heart like bits of gushing
 gore. . . .

VIII.

'Twas *he* said heads, not hearts, were made to
 break :
He taught me this that night in splendid scorn.
I learned too well. . . . The dance was done. Ere
 morn
We mounted — he and I — but no more
 spake. . . .
And this for woman's love! My lily worn
In her dark hair in pride, to then be torn
And trampled on, for this bold stranger's
 sake ! . . .
Two men rode silent back toward the lake;
Two men rode silent down — but only one
Rode up at morn to meet the rising sun.

    The walls are steep ;
    The crags shall keep

Their everlasting watch profound.
    The walls are steep,
    The waves are deep;
And if a dead man should be found
By red-clad fishers in their round,
Why, who shall say but he was drowned?

Lake Como, 1874.

A GARIBALDIAN'S STORY.

I.

" A Y, signor! that's Nervi, just under the
lights

That look down from the forts on the Genoese
heights ;

And that stone set in stone in the rim of the sea,

Like a tall figure rising and reaching a hand,

Marks the spot where the chief and his red-
shirted band

Hoisted sail. . . . Have a light? Ah, yes : as
for me

I have lights, and a leg — short a leg, as you see ;

And have three fingers hewn from this strong
sabre-hand.

II.

"See that cursèd cowled monk, black-mantled,
and black

In his heart as the plague, or the stole at his
back,

Stealing by like a spy down that sweet wooded
    way?

Well, these were the fellows we grappled.   Why
    they —

They were thick in the land as the locusts.
    The land

Was eaten alive by their indolence.   Yea,

They did toil not nor spin, and yet their array

Was as purple and gold; and they laid heavy
    hand

On the first of the fruits, of the flocks; and the
    gown

Soiled the first fairest maidens of country and
    town.

III.

" Look you there !   Do you see where the blue
    bended floors

Of the heavens are frescoed with stars?   See
    the heights,

Then the bent hills beneath, where the grape-
    growers' doors

Open out and look down in a crescent of lights?

Well, there I was born; grew tall.   Then the
    call

For bold men for Sicily.
        I rose from the vines,
Shook back my long hair, looked forth, then let
    fall
My dull pruning-hook, and stood full in the
    lines.
Then my young promised bride held her head
    to her breast
As a sword trailed the stones, and I strode with
    a zest.
But a sable-cowled monk girt his gown, and
    looked down
With a leer in her face, as I turned from the
    town.

IV.

" Then from yonder green hills bending down to
    the seas,
Grouping here, grouping there, in the gray olive
    trees,
We watched the slow sun ; slow saw him retire
At last in the sea, like a vast isle of fire.
Then the chief drew his sword :
            There was that in his air,
As the care on his face came and went and still
    came,

As he gazed out at sea, and yet gazed anywhere,
That meant more, signor, more than a peasant
  can say.
Then at last, when the stars in the soft-tempered
  breeze
Glowed red and grew large, as if fanned to a
  flame,
Lo! something shot up from a black-muffled ship
Deep asleep in the bay, like a star gone astray:
Then down, double quick, with the sword-hilt
  a-trip,
Came the troop with a zest, and — that stone
  tells the rest.

V.

" Hot times at Marsala! and then under Rome
It was hell sure enough, and a whole column fell
Like new vines in a frost.
                    Then year followed year,
Until, stricken and sere, at last I came home —
As the strife lulled a spell, came limping back
  here —
Stealing back to my home, limping up out of hell.
But we won, did we not? Won, I scarcely know
  what —

Yet the whole land is free from the Alps to the
    sea.
Ah! my young promised bride? Christ, that
    cuts! Why, I thought
That her face had gone by, like a dream that was
    not.

VI.

" What a presence was hers! What a throat,
    what a mouth!
Why, a mouth that Rossetti, the painter, had
    smiled
But to see; had caught it on canvas, had set his
    craft wild
With talk of his picture from Northland to
    South! —
A mouth that half opened as hungered for love,
That trusted all things; a mouth that went out
With daring and valor, that never knew doubt,
Yet was proud and as pure as that bent moon
    above. . . .

VII.

. . . " Yes, peaches must ripen and show the sun's
    red
In their time, I suppose, like the full of a rose;

And some one must pluck them, 'tis very well
    said,
As they swell and grow rich and look luscious to
    touch:
Yet I fancy some men, some fiends, must have
    much
To repent of: This reaching up rudely of hand
For the early sweet-fruits of a warm, careless
    land;
This plucking and biting of every sweet peach
Ere yet it is ripe and come well to its worth,
Then casting it down, and quite spoiled, to the
    reach
Of the swine and the things that creep close to
    the earth. . . .

VIII.

"But he died! Look you here. Stand aside.
    Yes, he died
Like a dog in a ditch. In that low battle-moat
He was found on a morn. The red line on his
    throat
They said was a rope. 'Bah! the one-fingered
    man
Might have done it,' said one.

　　　　　　　　　　Then I laughed till I cried
When the guard led me forth, and the judge sat
　　　to scan
My hands and my strength, and to question me
　　　sore :
' Why, what has the match-man to do with all
　　　this, —
The one-fingered man, with his life gone amiss ? '
I cried as I laughed, and they vexed me no more.

　　　.　　　.　　　.　　　.　　　.　　　.　　　.

Some men must fill trenches.　Ten thousand go
　　　down
As unnamed and unknown as the stones in a wall,
For the few to pass over and on to renown :
And I am of these.
　　　　　　　　The old king has his crown,
And my country is free ; and what more, after all,
Did I ask from the first ?
　　　　　　　　　Don't you think that yon lights
Through the black olive trees look divine on the
　　　seas ?
Then look you above, where the Apennines bend :
Why, you scarcely can tell, as you peer through
　　　the trees,
Where the great stars begin or the cottage-lights
　　　end !

IX.

" Yes, a little bit lonely, that can't be denied :
But as good place to wait for a sign as may be.
I shall watch on the shore, looking out as before ;
And the chief on his isle in the calm middle sea,
With his sword gathered up, stands waiting with
    me
For the great silent ship.
              We shall cross to the shore
Where a white city lies like yon Alps in the skies,
And look down on this sea ; and right well
    satisfied.

X.

"Ay! The whole country round vaunts our deed,
    and the town
Raised that shaft on the spot, — for the whole
    land is free ;
And some won renown, and one won a crown,
And one won a right to sell lights by the sea.
Have a light, sir, to-night? Ah, thanks, signor,
    thanks !
Bon voyage, bon voyage! Bless you and your
    francs."

GENOA, October, 1873.

THE IDEAL AND THE REAL.

PART I.

> " And full these truths eternal
> O'er the yearning spirit steal,
> That the real is the ideal,
> And the ideal is the real."

I.

SHE was damned with the dower of beauty. She
Had gold in shower about her brow.
Her feet!—why, her two blessed feet were so
small
They could nest in this hand. When she stood
up so tall,
So gracious, so grand, she was all to me,—
My present, my past, my eternity! . . .
She lives in my dreams. I behold her now
On that shoreless white river that flowed like a sea
At her feet where I sat. . . . How her lips pushed
out
In their brave, warm welcome of dimple and pout!

II.

'Twas eons agone.   By a river that ran
Fathomless, echoless, limitless, on,
And shoreless, and peopled with never a man, —
We met, soul to soul. . . . No land; yet I think
There were willows and lilies that leaned to drink.
The stars were all sealed and the moons were gone.
The wide shining circles that girdled that world,
They were distant and dim.   An incense curled
In vapory folds from that river that ran
All shoreless, with never the presence of man.

III.

How sensuous the night! how soft was the sound
Of her voice on the night!   How warm was her
     breath
In that world that had never yet tasted of death
Or forbidden sweet fruit! . . . In that far pro-
     found
We were camped on the edges of god-land.   We
Were the people of Saturn.   The watery fields,
The wide-winged, dolorous birds of the sea, —
They acknowledged but us.   Our battle-shields
Were my naked white palms; our food it was love.
Our roof was the fresco of stars above.

IV.

How tender she was, and how timid she was!
How turned she to me where that wide river ran,
With its lilies and willows and watery reeds,
And heeded as only your true love heeds! . . .
But a black-hoofed beast, with the head of a man,
Stole down where she sat at my side, and began
To puff his cheeks, then to play, then to pause,
With his double-reed pipe ; then to play and to play
As never played man since the world began,
And never shall play till the judgment day.

V.

How he puffed! how he played! Then adown
        the dim shore,
This half-devil man, all hairy and black,
Did dance with his hoofs in the sand, looking back
As his song died away. . . . She turned never more
Unto me after that. She arose, and she pass'd
Right on from my sight. Then I followed as fast
As a love could follow. But ever before
Like a spirit she fled. How vain and how far
Did I follow my beauty from star to white star!
From foamy white sea, and from stormy black
        shore.

VI.

But I here shall abide. I shall pipe on a reed.
I shall sit by the waters my whole life through.
I shall sing wild songs. I shall take no heed
Of the things forbidden, or of bitter-sweet fruit.
I shall feast with the gods. I shall sing for the few.
I shall pipe not for love. I shall reach my hand,
And pluck fair lilies from the bank by the root.
I shall laugh like a satyr. I shall dance on the sand,
I shall rove o'er the sea, I shall rest by the shore;
But never seek love upon earth any more.

VII.

Never more upon earth! Yet the heaven-bound
     span
Of life upon earth, — lo, it is but to-day!
Last night was the land that remembers no man,
To-morrow the skies! . . . Then who shall
     gainsay
The valor of patience? Lo! there I shall woo
In the gardens of God, on the centremost star
Of all whirling stars. Face front I shall view
This one splendid face I have followed so far.
There love shall heal love of her hard battle-scars,
Begun on the outermost edge of the stars.

VIII.

How long I had sought her! My soul of fire
It had fed on itself. I fasted, I cried;
Was tempted by many. Yet still I denied
The touch of all things, and kept my desire. . . .
I stood by the lion of St. Mark in that hour
Of Venice, when gold of the sunset is rolled
From cloud to cathedral, to turret and tower,
In matchless, magnificent garment of gold.
Then I knew she was near; yet I had not known
Her form or her face since the stars were sown.

IX.

We two had been parted — God pity us! — when
The stars were unnamed and all heaven was
  . dim;
We two had been parted far back on the rim
And the outermost border of heaven's red bars;
We two had been parted ere the meeting of men,
Or God had set compass on spaces as yet;
We two had been parted ere God had set
His finger to spinning the purple with stars, —
And now, at the last in the gold and set
Of the sun of Venice, we two had met.

X.

Where the lion of Venice, with brows a-frown,
With toss'd mane tumbled, and teeth in air,
Looks out in his watch o'er the watery town,
With a paw half lifted, with his claws half bare,
By the blue Adriatic, in the edge of the sea, —
I saw her.   I knew her, but she knew not me.
I had found her at last !   Why, I had sailed
The antipodes through, had sought, had hailed
'All flags, had climbed where the storm-clouds
    curled,   [world.
And called through the awful arched dome of the

XI.

I saw her one moment, then fell back abashed,
And filled full to the throat. . . . Then I turned
   me once more
So glad to the sea, while the level sun flashed
On the far, snowy Alps. . . . Her breast ! — why,
   her breast
Was white as twin pillows that allure you to rest ;
Her sloping limbs moved like to melodies, told
As she rose from the sea ; and she threw back
   the gold
Of her glorious hair, and set face to the shore. . . .
I knew her !   I knew her, though we had not met
Since the far stars sang to the sun's first set.

XII.

How long I had sought her! I had hungered,
    nor ate
Of any sweet fruits. I had tasted not one
Of all the fair glories grown under the sun.
I had sought only her. Yea, I knew that she
Had come upon earth, and stood waiting for me
Somewhere by my way. But the pathways of fate.
They had led otherwhere ; the round world round,
The far North seas and the near profound
Had failed me for aye. Now I stood by that sea
Where ships drave by, and all dreamily.

XIII.

I had turned from the lion a time, and when
I looked tow'rd the tide and out on the lea
Of the town where the warm sea tumbled and
    teemed
With beauty, I saw her ! I knew her then,
The tallest, the fairest fair daughter of men.
Oh, Venice stood full in her glory. She gleamed
In the splendor of sunset and sensuous sea ;
Yet I saw but my bride, my all to me,
While the doves hurried home to the dome of
    Saint Mark,   [in the dark.
And the brass horses plunged their high manes

XIV.

I spake not, but caught at my breath ; I did raise
My face to fair heaven, to give God praise
That at last, ere the ending of time, we two
Had touched upon earth at the same sweet
    place. . . .
Yea, we never had met upon earth at all ;
Never, since ages ere Adam's fall,
Had we two met in the fulness of soul,
Where two are as one, but had wandered on
    through
The spheres, divided, where planets roll
Unnam'd and in darkness through limitless space.

XV.

Was it well with my love ? Was she true ?
    Was she brave
With virtue's own valor ? Was she waiting for
    me ?
Oh, how fared my love ? Had she home ? Had
    she bread ?
Had she known but the touch of the warm-
    tempered wave ?
Was she born upon earth with a crown on her
    head,

Or born, like myself, but a dreamer instead?
So long it had been! So long! Why the sea —
That wrinkled and surly, old, time-tempered
    slave —
Had been born, had his revels, grown wrinkled
    and hoar
Since I last saw my love on that uttermost shore.

XVI.

Oh, how fared my love? Once I lifted my face,
And I shook back my hair and looked out on the
    sea;
I pressed my hot palms as I stood in my place,
And cried: " Oh, I come like a king to your side
Though all hell intervene!" . . . "Hist! she
    may be a bride,
A mother at peace, with sweet babes on her
    knee!
A babe at her breast and a spouse at her side! —
Have I wandered too long, and has Destiny
Set mortal between us?" I buried my face
In my hands, and I moaned as I stood in my
    place.

XVII.

'Twas her year to be young. She was tall, she
   was fair —
Was she pure as the snow on the Alps over there?
'Twas her year to be young. She was fair, she
   was tall;
And I felt she was true, as I lifted my face
And saw her press down her rich robe to its place,
With a hand white and small as a babe's with a
   doll.
And her feet! — why, her feet in the white shin-
   ing sand
Were so small, 'twas a wonder the maiden could
   stand.
Then she pushed back her hair with a round
   hand that shone
And flashed in the light with a white starry stone.

XVIII.

Then, my love she is rich! My love she is fair!
Is she pure as the snow on the Alps over there?
She is gorgeous with wealth! " Thank God, she
   has bread,"
I said to myself. Then I humbled my head

In gratitude.   Then I questioned me where
Was her palace, her parents ?   What name did
    she bear ?
What mortal on earth came nearest her heart ?
Who touched the small hand till it thrilled to a
    smart ?
'Twas her year to be young.   She was proud,
    she was fair —
Was she pure as the snow on the Alps over there ?

XIX.

Beneath her blue robe her round bosom rose
In sensuous beauty !   She was white as the
    snows
Of the Tyrolese Alps.   Oh, the slope of her arm !
Oh, the rounded limbs' length !   The breasts
    heaving warm
As welcomes of love !   The lips pushing out !
The proud mouth gathered in dimple and pout !
Then the dusky depressions, suggestions of night,
They did make her pure whiteness but appear
    the more white :
Whiter indeed than the white soul of man,
Or the whitest marbles of the Vatican.

XX.

She loosened her robe that was blue like the sea,
And silken and soft as a babe's new born.
And my heart it leapt light as the sunlight at
    morn
At the sight of my love in her purity,
As she rose like a Naiad half-robed from the sea.
As careless, as calm as a queen can be,
She loosed and let fall all the raiment of blue,
·As she drew a white robe in a melody
Of her moving white limbs; and between the
    two,
Like a rift in a cloud, shone her fair form thro'.

XXI.

Now she turned, reached a hand; then a tall
    gondolier
Who had leaned on his oar, like a long lifted spear,
Shot sudden and swift and all silently,
And drew to her side as she turned from the
    tide . . .
It was odd, such a thing, and I counted it queer
That a princess like this, whether virgin or bride,

Should abide thus apart, and should bathe in that
    sea ;
And I shook back my hair, and so unsatisfied !
Then I fluttered the doves that were perched
    close about,
As I strode up and down in dismay and in doubt.

XXII.

Then she stood in the boat on the borders of
    night
As a goddess might stand on that far wonder-land
Of eternal sweet life, which men have named
    Death.
I turned to the sea, and I caught at my breath
As she crouched in the boat, and her white
    baby hand
Held her vestment of purple imperial and white.
Then the gondola shot, — swift, sharp from the
    shore :
There was never the sound of a song or of oar,
But the doves hurried home in white clouds to
    Saint Mark,
Where the lion looms high o'er the sea in the
    dark.

XXIII.

Then I cried: " Quick ! Follow her ! Follow
    her ! Fast !
Come, thrice double fare if you follow her true
To her own palace door !" There was plashing
    of oar
And rattle of rowlock. . . . I sat leaning low,
Looking far in the dark, looking out as we sped
With my soul all alert, bending down, leaning low.
But only the oaths of the men as we pass'd,
When we jostled them sharp as we sudden shot
    thro'
The watery town. Then a deep, distant roar —
The rattle of rowlock, the rush of the oar.

XXIV.

We rock'd and we rode: then the oars keeping pace
Gave stroke for short stroke in the swift stormy
    chase.
I lifted my face, and lo ! fitfully
The heavens breathed lightning : it did lift and fall
As if angels were parting God's curtains. Then
    deep
And indolent-like and as if half-asleep,

As if half made angry to move at all,
The thunder moved.   It confronted me.
It stood like an avalanche poised on a hill :
I saw its black brows.   I heard it stand still.

XXV.

Then we flew by a great house hurriedly,
With its four walls washed by the foamy sea ;
'Twas the place where Shelley was wont to be.
I heard in the heavens the howlings of men ;
High up in the dark I did hear men shout ;
And I lifted my eyes as the lightnings fell,
And I saw hands thrust through the bars ; and then
I knew 'twas the madhouse howling at me :
So doleful, so lone !   Like a land cast out,
And awful as Lucifer throned in hell.

XXVI.

Then an oath.   Then a prayer.   Then a gust
     that made rents
Thro' the yellow-sailed fishers.   Then suddenly
Came sharp-forked fire !   Then far thunder fell
Like the great first gun ! Ah, then there was rout
Of ships like the breaking of regiments,
And shouts as if hurled from an upper hell.

Then tempest! It lifted, it spun us about,
Then shot us ahead through the hills of the sea
As if a great arrow shot shoreward in wars —
Then heaven split open till we saw the blown
  stars.

XXVII.

On! On! through the foam, through the storm,
  through the town.
She was gone! She was lost in the wilderness
Of palaces lifting their marbles of snow.
I stood in my gondola. Up and all down
I pushed through the surge of the salt-flood street
Above me, below. . . . 'Twas only the beat
Of the sea's sad heart. . . . Then I heard below
The water-rat building, and nothing but that;
Not even the sea-bird screaming distress,
As she lost her way in that wilderness.

XXVIII.

I listened all night. I caught at each sound;
I clutched and I caught as a man that drown'd —
Only the sullen, low growl of the sea
Far out the flood-street at the edge of the ships.
Only the billow slow licking his lips,

Like a dog that lay crouching there watching for
    me,
Growling and showing white teeth all the night,
Reaching his neck and as ready to bite.
Only the waves with their salt-flood tears
Fawning white stones of a thousand years.

XXIX.

Only the birds in the loftiness
Of column and dome and of glittering spire
That thrust to heaven and held the fire
Of the thunder still ; the bird's distress
As he struck his wings in that wilderness,
On marbles that speak and thrill and inspire. —
The night below and the night above ;
The water-rat building, the startled white dove ;
The wide-winged, dolorous sea-bird's call,
The water-rat building, — but that was all.

XXX.

Silent and slowly, and up and down,
I rowed and I rowed me for many an hour,
By beetling palace and toppling tower,
In the dark and the deep of the watery town.

Only the water-rat building by stealth,
Only the sea-bird astray in his flight
As he struck his wings in the clouds of night,
On spires that sprang from old Adria's wealth,
On marbles that move with their eloquence,
On statues so sweeter than utterance.

XXXI.

Lo! pushing the darkness from pillar to post,
The morning came silent and gray like a ghost
Slow up the canal. I leaned from the prow
And listened. Not even the bird in distress
Screaming above through the wilderness;
Not even the stealthy old water-rat now.
Only the bell in the fisherman's tower,
Slow tolling at sea and telling the hour
To kneel to their sweet Santa Barbara
For tawny fishers at sea and pray.

THE IDEAL AND THE REAL.

PART II.

I.

HIGH over my head, carved cornice, quaint
　　spire ;
And ancient-built palaces knocked their gray
　　brows
Together and frowned. The slow-creeping scows
Scraped the wall on each side. High over, the
　　fire
Of sudden-born morning came flaming in bars :
While up through my chasm I could count the
　　stars.　　　　　　　　　　　　　[death
My God ! Such damp ruin ! The dank smell of
Came up the canal : I could scarce take my breath !
'Twas the fit place for pirates, for women who keep
Contagion of body and soul where they sleep.

II.

Great heaven! A white hand did beckon to me
From an old mouldy door, and almost in my reach.
I sprang to the sill as one wrecked to a beach;
I sprang with wide arms: it was she! it was
　she! . . .
In such a damn'd place! And what was her trade?
To think I had followed, so faithful, so far,
From eternity's brink, from star to white star,
To find her, to find her, nor wife nor sweet maid!
To find her a shameless poor creature of shame,
A nameless lost body, men hardly dare name.

III.

All alone in her pride, on that damp dismal floor
She stood to entice me. I bowed me before
All-conquering beauty. I called her my queen.
I told her my love as I would have told
My love had I found her as pure as gold.
I reached her my hand, as fearless a man
As man fronting cannon. I cried: " Come forth
To the sun! There are lands to the south, to
　the north,
Anywhere where you will. Dash the shame
　from your brow;
Come with me, for ever; and come with me now!"

IV.

Why, I had turned pirate for her! I had seen
Tall ships burned from seas, like to stubble from
    field.   .   [yield,
I would not now forsake her. Why should I now
When she needed me most? Had I found her a
    queen,
And beloved by the world, — why, what had I
    done?
I had wooed her, and wooed her, and wooed till I
    won!
Then, if I had loved her with gold and fair fame,
Would not I now love her, and love her the same?
My soul hath a pride. I would tear out my heart
And feed it to dogs, could it play such a part.

V.

I told her all things. Her brow took a frown;
Her grand Titan beauty, so tall, so serene,
The one perfect woman, mine own idol queen!
Her proud swelling bosom it broke up and down:
Then she spake, and she shook in her soul as she
    said,
With her small hands upheld to her bent, aching
    head: .

"Go back to the world! go back and alone,
Thou strange, stormy soul, intense as mine
　　own!"
I said : "I will wait! I will wait in the pass
Of death, until Time he shall break his glass!

VI.

"Don't you know me, my bride of the white
　　worlds before?
Why, don't you remember the white milky-way
Of stars, that we traversed a life-time through?
We were counting the colors, we were naming
　　the seas
Of the vaster ones. You remember the trees
That swayed in the cloudy white heavens, and
　　bore
Bright crystals of sweets, and the sweet manna-
　　dew?
Why, you smile as you weep, and you lift up
　　your brow,
And your bright eyes speak, and you know me
　　now!
You know me as if 'twere but yesterday!

VII.

"Now here in the lands where the gods did love,
Where the white Europa was won, — she rode
Her milk-white bull through these same warm
　　seas, —
Yea, here in the lands where the Hercules,
With the lion's heart and the heart of the dove,
Did walk in his naked great strength, and strode
In the sensuous air with his lion's skin
Flapping and fretting his knotted thews ;
Where Theseus did wander, and Jason cruise, —
Lo! here let the life of all lives begin.

VIII.

" Lo ! here where the Orient balms blow in,
Where heaven is kindest, where all God's blue
Seems a great gate opened to welcome you, —
Come, rise and go forth, and forget your sin !"
Then rose her great heart, so grander far
Than I had believed on that outermost star ;
And she put by her tears, and calmly she said,
With hands held low and with bended head :
" Go thou through the doors of death, and wait
For me on the innermost side of the gate.

IX.

"It is breaking my heart; but, 'tis best," she said.
"Thank God that this life is but a day's span,
But a wayside inn for weary, worn man —
A night and a day; and, to-morrow, the spell
Of darkness is broken.   Now, darling, farewell!
Nay, touch not the hem of my robe! — it is red
With sins that your own sex heaped on my head!
But go, love, go!   Yet remember this plan,
That whoever dies first is to sit down and wait
Inside death's door, and watch at the gate."

X.

Then I grew noble.   Yea, I grew so tall
I could almost reach to the golden hair
Of that poor, pitiful Cyprian there.
I did let my mantle of self-love fall,
And I stood all naked, so weak, so small,
I wondered that I could ever now dare
Lift up my prayer to Heaven at all. . . .
And I accepted her lesson.   I said,
With hands clasped down and declining head,
"I will go, I will wait by the gates of the dead.

XI.

" And you, O woman ! go patient on through
The course that man hath compelled you to.
Then back to your mother, the earth, my love ;
Go, press to her bosom your beautiful brow,
Till it blends with your clay, and so purifies
Your flesh of the stains that so sully it now :
Lie down in the loam, the populous loam,
Yea, sleep for the eons with death ; then rise
As white, as light as the wings of a dove, —
And so made holy, oh love, come home !

XII.

" Farewell for all time ! And now," I said,
" What thing upon earth have I left to do ?
Why, I shall go down through the gates of the
        dead,
And wait for your coming your long life thro' —
As you have commanded, lo ! I shall obey.
I shall sit, I shall wait for you, love, alway ;
Shall wait by the side of the gate for you,
Waiting, and counting the days as I wait ;
Shall wait as that beggar that sat by the gate
Of Jerusalem, waiting the Judgment Day."

Venice, 1874.

IL CAPUCIN.

I.

ONLY a basket for fruits or bread
     And the bits you divide with your dog,
  which you
Had left from your dinner. The round year
     through
He never once smiles. He bends his head
To the scorn of men. He gives the road
To the grave ass groaning beneath his load.
He is ever alone. Lo ! never a hand
Is laid in his hand through the whole wide land,
Save when a man dies, and he shrives him home.
And that is the Capucin monk of Rome.

II.

He coughs, he is humped, and he hobbles about
In sandals of wood. Then a hempen cord
Girdles his loathsome gown. Abhorred !
Ay ! lonely, indeed, as a leper cast out.
One gown in three years ! and — bah ! how he
     smells !

He slept last night in his coffin of stone,
This monk that coughs, this skin and bone,
This living corpse from the damp cold cells.
Yet, up in the morn, come storm or shine,
And forth at four to wail at the shrine.

III.

Go ye where the Pincian, half-levelled down,
The sixth of the seven rent hills of Rome,
Slopes slow to the south. These men in brown
Have a monkery there, quaint, builded of stone ;
And, living or dead, 'tis the brown men's home,
These dead brown monks that are living in Rome !

IV.

You will hear wood sandals on the sounding floor,
A cough, then the lift of a latch, then the door
Groans open, and horror ! Four walls of stone
Are gorgeous with flowers and frescos of bone !
There are bones in the corners and bones on the
    wall ;
And he barks like a dog that watches his bone,
This monk in brown from his bed of stone —
Yea, barks, and he coughs, and that is all.

V.

At last he will cough as if up from his cell;
Will strut with considerable pride about,
Will lead through his flowers of bone, and smell
Their odors; then talk, as he points them out,
Of the virtues and deeds of the gents who wore
The respective bones but the year before.

Then he thaws at last, ere the bones are through,
And talks and talks as he turns them about
And stirs up a most uncomfortable smell;
Yea, talks of his brown dead brothers, till you
Wish them, as they are no doubt, in — well,
A very deep well. . . . And that may be why,
As he shows you the door and bows good-by,
That he bows so low for a franc or two,
To shrive their souls and to get them out —
These bony brown men who have their home,
Dead or alive, in their cells in Rome.

VI.

What good does he do in the world? Ah! well,
Now that is a puzzler. . . . But, listen! He
    prays.
His life is the fast of the forty days.

And then, when the thief and the beggar fell
And had died in the way; when the plague
    came down, —
Christ! who was it cried to these men in brown
When other men fled?   And what man was
    seen
Stand firm to the death but the Capucin?

ROME, 1873.

FAITH.

I.

FORTY days and forty nights,
    Blown about the broken waters,
Noah, and his sons and daughters;
Forty days they beat and blow —
Forty days of faith, and lo!
    The olive leaf, the lifted heights,
    The rest at last, the calm delights.

II.

Forty years of sun and sand,
Serpents, beasts, and wilderness,
Desolation and distress,
War and famine, wail and woe —
Forty years of faith, and lo!
    The mighty Moses lifts a hand
    And shows at last the Promised Land.

III.

Forty days to fast and pray,
The patient Christ outworn defied
The angry tempter at his side.
Forty days or forty years
Of patient sacrifice and tears —
    Lo ! what are all of these the day
    That Time has nothing more to say ?

IV.

Lift your horns, exult and blow,
Believe and labor.   Tree and vine
Must flourish, ere the fruit and wine
Reward your planting.   Round and round
The rocky walls, with faith profound,
    The trumpets blew ; blew loud, and lo !
    The tumbled walls of Jericho.

MILAN, 1873.

TO FLORENCE.

I.

IF all God's world a garden were,
   And women were but flowers;
If men were bees that busied there .
Through all the summer hours, —
Oh! I would hum God's garden through,
For honey, till I came to you.

II.

Then I should hive within your hair,
Its sun and gold together;
And I should bide in glory there,
Through all the changeful weather.
Oh! I should sip but one, this one
Sweet flower underneath the sun.

III.

Oh! I would be a king, and coin
Your golden hair for money;
And I would only have to seek
Your lips for hoards of honey.
Oh! I would be the richest king
That ever wore a signet-ring.

FLORENCE, 1874.

FOR PAULINE.

I.

LOVE me, love, but breathe it low,
  Soft as summer weather;
If you love me, tell me so,
  As we sit together,
Sweet and still as roses blow:
Love me, love, but breathe it low.

II.

Tell me only with your eyes,
  Words are cheap as water,
If you love me, looks and sighs
  Tell my mother's daughter
More than all the world may know:
Love me, love, but breathe it low.

III.

Words for others, storm and snow,
　Wind and changeful weather —
Let the shallow waters flow
　Foaming on together ;
But love is still and deep, and oh !
Love me, love, but breathe it low.

Pieve di Cadora, 1873.

TO CARRIE A. S.

I.

THE sea-dove some twin shadow has,
　　The lark has loves in seas of grass,
The wild beast trumpets back his vow,
The squirrel laughs along his bough ;
But I, I am as lone, alas !
As yon white moon when white clouds pass !
　　As lonely and unloved, alas !
　　As clouds that weep and droop and pass.

II.

Oh, maiden ! singing over sweet
At cottage door, in field of corn,
Where woodbines twine for thy retreat —
Sing sweet through all thy summer morn.
For love is landing at thy feet,
On isle of vine, in seas of corn.
　　But I, I am unloved and lorn,
　　As winter winds of winter morn.

III.

The ships, black-bellied, climb the sea,
The seamen seek their loves on land,
And love and lover, hand in hand,
Go singing, glad as glad can be.
But never more shall love seek me
By breezy sea or broken land.

By broken wild or willow tree,
Nay, never more shall love seek me.

Naples, 1872.

THE UNKNOWN TONGUE.

I.

THAT baby, I knew her in days of old.
　　You doubt that I lived in a land made fair
With many soft moons, and was mated there?
Now mark you! I saw but to-day on the street
A sweet girl-baby, whose delicate feet
As yet upon earth took but uncertain hold;
Yet she carried a doll, and she toddled alone,
And she talked to that doll in a tongue her own.
The sweet little stranger! why, her face still bore
The look of the people from her far star-shore.

II.

Ah! you doubt me still? Then listen: While you
Have looked to the earth for gold, why I —
I have looked to the steeps of the starry sky.
And which, indeed, had the fairer view

Of the infinite things, the dreamer or you? . . .
How blind be men when they will not see !
If men must look in the dust, or look,
At best, with the eyes bound down to a book,
Why, who shall deny that it comes to me
To sail white ship through the ether sea? ·

III.

Yea, I am a dreamer.   Yet while you dream,
Then I am awake.   When a child, back through
The gates of the past I peered, and I knew
The land I had lived in.   I saw a broad stream ;
Saw rainbows that compassed a world in their
      reach ;
I saw my belovèd go down on the beach ;
Saw her lean to this earth, saw her looking for me
As shipmen look from their ships at sea. . . .
The sweet girl-baby !   Why, that unknown
      tongue
Is the tongue she has talked since the stars were
      young.

Naples, 1873.

UNICA-ÆTERNA.

I.

I DREAMED, O Queen, of thee last night;
  I can but dream of thee to-day.
But dream? Oh! I could kneel and pray
To one, who, like a tender light,
Leads ever on my lonesome way,
And will not pass — yet will not stay.

II.

I dreamed, O Princess, regal Queen,
That I had followed thee afar,
And faithful, as my polar star;
But then, as now, I had not seen
The day I dared draw near to thee,
But followed, worshipped, silently.

III.

I dreamed we roamed in elden land;
I saw you walk in splendid state,
With lifted head and heart elate,
And lilies in your white right hand,

Beneath the proud Saint Peter's dome
That, silent, lords almighty Rome.

v.

A diamond star was in your hair,
Your garments were of gold and snow;
And men did turn and marvel so,
And men did say, How matchless fair!
And all men followed as you pass'd;
But I came silent, lone, and last.

v.

And holy men in sable gown,
And girt with cord, and sandal shod,
Did look to thee, and then to God.   [down;
They crossed themselves, with heads held
They chid themselves, in fear that they
Should, seeing thee, forget to pray.

VI.

Men pass'd, men spake in wooing word;
Men pass'd, ten thousand in a line.
You stood before the sacred shrine,
You stood as if you had not heard.
And then you turned in calm command,
And laid two lilies in my hand.

VII.

O Lady, if by sea or land
You yet might weary of all men,
And turn unto your singer then,
And lay one lily in his hand, —
Lo! I would follow true and far
As seamen track the polar star.

VIII.

My soul is young, my heart is strong;
• O Lady, reach a hand to-day,
And thou shalt walk the milky-way,
For I will give thy name to song.
Lo! I am of the kings of thought,
And thou shalt live when kings are not.

IX.

Oh, reach a hand, your hand in mine!
Why, I could sing as never man
Has sung since prophecy began!
And thou should'st be both song and shrine....
And yet I falter in thy sight,
And dare not breathe the thought I write.

SIROCCO.

I.

THERE were black clouds crossing the Alps, and they
Rolled straight upon Venice.   Then far away,
As if catching new breath and gathering strength
In the Ægean hills, on the pall of the day,
Stood the terrible Thunder.   Then hip and thigh
He smote all heaven, and the lightning leapt
Like red swords thrust through the night full
    length —
Swords thrust through the black heart of night
    as he slept!
Then ribbon and skein kept threading the sky;
Then, ere you scarcely had time to think,
The sea lay darkling and black as ink.

II.

Then many a sail, tri-colored, and cross'd
By the lone sad cross of Calvary,
Drove by us and dwindled to blinding specks;
Drove straight in the grinning white teeth of the
    sea,
Like lonesome spirits, forlorn and lost.
Then a ship with my stars of the West! and then
There were golden crescents, tall turbaned men
All silent and devil-like keeping the decks;
Then hearse-like gondolas hurried about,
As if sniffing the storm with their lifted snout.

VENICE, 1874.

PACE IMPLORA.

I.

BETTER it were to abide by the sea,
   Loving somebody, and satisfied ;
Better it were to grow babes on the knee,
To anchor you down for all your days,
Than to wander and wander in all these ways,
Land-forgotten and love-denied.
Yea, better to live as the mountaineers live,
Than entreat of the gods what they will not give.

II.

Better sit still where born, I say,
Wed one sweet woman and love her well,
Love and be loved in the old East way,
Drink sweet waters, and dream in a spell,
Than to wander in search of the Blessed Isles,
And to sail the thousands of watery miles
In the search of love, and find you at last
On the edge of the world, and a curs'd outcast.

III.

Yea, laugh with your neighbors, live in their way
Be it never so humble.   The humbler the home,
The braver, indeed, to brunt the fray.
Share their delights and divide your tears,
Love and be loved for the full round years,
As men once loved in the young world's pride,
Ere men knew madness and came to roam, —
When they lived where their fathers had lived
        and died,
Lived and so loved for a thousand years.

IV.

Better it were for the world, I say,
Better indeed for a man's own good,
That he should sit still where he was born,
Be it land of sand, or of oil and corn,
White sea-border or great black wood,
Bleak white winter or bland sweet May, —
Than to wander the world, as I have done,
For the one dear woman that is under the sun.

V.

Better abide, though·the skies be dun,
And the rivers espoused of the ice and snow ;
Better abide, though the thistles grow,
And the city of smoke be obscured of the sun,
Than to seek red poppies and the sweet dream-
    land —
Than to wander the world as I to-day,
Breaking the heart into bits like clay,
And leaving it scattered upon every hand.

    VENICE, 1874.

ALONE.

I.

I AM as lone as lost winds on the height;
　As lone as yonder leaning moon at night,
That climbs, like some sad noiseless-footed nun,
Far up against the steep and starry height,
As if on holy mission. Yea, as one
That knows no ark, or isle, or resting-place,
Or chronicle of time, or wheeling sun,
I drive for ever on through endless space.
Like some lone bird in everlasting flight,
My lonesome soul sails on through lonesome seas
　　of night.

II.

Alone in sounding hollows of the sea;
Alone on lifted, heaving hills of foam:
To never rest; to ever rise and roam
Where never kind or kindred soul may be;

To roam where ships of commerce never ride,
Sail on, and so forget the rest of shore ;
To hear the waves complain, as.if they died ;
To see the vast waves heave for evermore ;
To know that no ships cross or measure these,
My shoreless, chartless, strange, and most un-
   common seas.

CADORA, 1873.

IMPLORA.

I.

OH! who art thou, veiled shape? My soul
    cries out
Through mist and storm.   Lean thou to me!
Come nearer, thou, that I may feel and see
Thy wounded side, and so forget all doubt!
How terrible the night!   I kneel to thee;
I clasp thy knees; would clamber to thy hair.
As one shipwrecked on some broad, broken sea,
Through intermingled oaths and awful shout,
Uplifts white hands and prays in his despair, —
So now my curses break into a prayer.

   BELLAGIO, 1874.

THE QUEST OF LOVE.

I.

BEHOLD! my quest has brought but rue
    and rime!
I loved the blushing, bounding, singing Spring:
She scarce would pause a day to hear me sing.
I loved her sister, gorgeous, golden Summer-
    time:
She gathered close her robes and rustled past,
Through yellow fields of corn. She scorned to
    cast
One tender look of love or hope behind;
But, sighing, died upon the Autumn wind.
Oh, then I loved the vast, the lonesome Night:
She, too, passed on in scorn, and perished from
    my sight.

II.

Oh! lives there nought on all the girdled world,
That may survive one day its sorry birth?
The very Moon grows thin and hunger-curled;
The ardent Sun forgets his love of Earth,

And turns, dark-browed, and draws his reached
  arms back,
The while she, mourning, moves on, clad in
  black.
But list! I once did hear the good priest tell
That hell is everlasting. Oh, my friend,
To know that there is aught that may not end!
Now let us kneel and give God thanks that hell
  is hell.

LAKE COMO, August, 1873.

O LOVE!

I.

THE long days through I sit and sigh, alas!
   For love! Lone, beggar-like, beside the
    way
I sit forlorn in lanes where Day must pass.
I stretch imploring palms toward the Day,
And cry, " O Day! but give me love! I die
For love! I let all other gifts go by.
Yea, bring me but one love that runs to waste,
One love that men pass by in heedless haste,
And I will kiss thy feet and ask no more
From all To-morrow's rich, mysterious store."

II.

The drear days mock me in my mute request ;
The dark years roll like breakers on the shore,
And die in futile thunder. As in jest,
They bring bright, empty shells, — bring nothing
   more.

Oh, say ! is sweet Love dead and hid from all
Who would disdain a colder touch than his?
Then show me where Love lies. Put back the
    pall.
Lo ! I will fall upon his face and kiss
Sweet Love to life again; or I will lie,
Lamenting, prone beside his dust, and die.

ANCONA, 1874.

AFTER THE BOAR HUNT.

I.

'TWERE better blow trumpets 'gainst love, keep away
That traitorous urchin with fire or shower,
Or fair or foul means you may have in your power,
Than have him come near you for one little hour.
Take physic, consult with your doctor, as you
Would fight a contagion ; carry all through
The populous day some drug that smells loud,
As you pass on your way, or make way through the crowd.
Talk war, or carouse : only keep off the day
Of his coming, with every true means in your way.

II.

Blow smoke in the eyes of the world, and laugh
With the broad-chested men, as you loaf at your
    inn,
As you crowd to your inn from your saddles,
    and quaff
The red wine from a horn; while your dogs at
    your feet,
Your slim spotted dogs, like the fawn, and as
    fleet,
Crouch patiently by and look up at your face,
As they wait for the call of the horn to the
    chase:
For you shall not suffer, and you shall not sin,
Until peace goes out and till love comes in.

III.

Love horses and hounds, meet many good men —
Yea, men are most proper, and keep you from
    care.
There is strength in a horse. There is pride in
    his will:
It is sweet to look back as you climb the steep hill.

There is room.   You have movement of limb ;
   you have air,
Have the smell of the wood, of the grasses : and
   then
What comfort to rest, as you lie thrown at
   length
All night and alone, with your fists full of
   strength !

   Turin, 1874.

DOLCE FAR NIENTE.

I.

A H, how one wanders! Yet after it all,
   When you really have nought of account
      to say,
It is better, perhaps, to pull leaves by the way;
See the wide moons ride, or the small stars fall,
Nor keep down to the earth with the dust on
      the feet,
Upon time-worn levels that do tire one
With very perfection of rest and retreat,
That the great world walks all the days of the sun.

II.

And then, too, in Venice! dear moth-eaten town;
One palace of pictures; great frescos spilled down
Outside of the walls from the fulness thereof:
How can one go on? Let laugh and let scoff;
Sit down by my side and let all time pass.

By the tranquil bride of the tranquil seas,
By the white bride born of steel and of storm,
And of iron-footed old tyrannies,
We two will sit; and her beautiful form
Shall shine in the sea as her bridal glass.

VENICE, 1873.

TO THE LION OF SAINT MARK.

I.

I KNOW you, lion of gray Saint Mark;
　　You fluttered the seas beneath your wing,
Were king of the seas with never a king.
Now over the deep and up in the dark,
High over the girdles of bright gas-light,
With wings in the air as if for flight,
And crouching as if about to spring
From top of your granite of Africa, —
Say, what shall be said of you some day?

II.

What shall be said, O grim Saint Mark,
Savage old beast so crossed and churled,
By the after men from the under-world?
What shall be said as they search along
And sail these seas for some sign or spark
Of the old dead fires of the dear old days,
When men and story have gone their ways,
Or even your city and name from song?

III.

Why, sullen old monarch of stilled Saint Mark,
Strange men of the West, wise-mouthed and
strong,
Will come some day and, gazing long
And mute with wonder, will say of thee:
" This is the Saint!   High over the dark,
Foot on the bible and great teeth bare,
Tail whipped back and teeth in the air —
Lo! this is the Saint, and none but he ! "

VENICE, 1873.

TO THE LION OF ST. MARK AGAIN.

I.

SPHINX-LIKE lion, art prophet, or what?
    Nay, Noah or prophet art thou of St. Mark.
But, king of the desert or slave of the sea,
What thou hast been or what shalt be,
What thou art now or what art not,
In city at sea or darkling ark, —
Lead us and land us on some sweet shore,
Some new-washed summit where olives are green,
And never the visage of sorrow is seen ˙
For ever and ever and evermore:

II.

To the Isles of the Blest by the Isles of Greece,
And on and beyond, where the great moon's face
Bends low and large to the golden grain
The whole year through; where death nor pain,
Nor any loud thought has name or place, —
To the land of olives, to the land of peace.
Lead us and land us, oh that were best,
To the land of love and the land of rest.

III.

Is there rest upon earth?   Ah, brazen king,
Set a-top of the town with glittering wing,
Say! King of Assyria, set king of the sea,
Now what do you read from the prophecy?
And what says thy book? And what were best?
Oh say, from thy pulpit set high in the air,
When is the harvest of love and where?
And where is the land, and when is the rest?

IV.

Floating in flood of salt sea-foam,
· And seeking for what?   For the golden fleece?
For the land of giants?   For the sea-lost moon?
For the land of eternal afternoon?
Or the gates of Hell or of Hercules?
Oh! wrinkled old lion that tops Saint Mark,
A home on the seas were never a home.
Lo! here are the doves, let this be the ark:
Now where is the olive, and when is the peace?

VENICE, 1874.

UNDER THE LION OF SAINT MARK
AT NIGHT.

I.

O TERRIBLE lion of tamed Saint Mark!
 Tamed old lion with the tumbled mane
Toss'd to the clouds and lost in the dark,
With high-held wings and tail whipped back,
Foot on the bible as if thy track
Led thee the lord of the seas again, —
Say, what of thy watch o'er the watery town?
Say, what of the worlds walking up and down?

II.

O silent old monarch that tops Saint Mark,
That sat thy throne for a thousand years,
That lorded the deep, that defied all men, —
Lo! I see visions at sea in the dark;

8

And I see something that shines like tears,
And I hear something that sounds like sighs,
And I hear something that sounds as when
A great soul suffers and sinks and dies.

VENICE, 1873.

TO SANTA BARBARA OF VENICE.

I.

WHERE is my beauty? Oh where is my
  bride
Of the old dim days ere the gleaming snows
Sat tent on the Alps? The poppies red
In the golden days were my bridal bed.
Oh, bring me my bride where the white sea flows,
And the yellow sail blows to the Lido's side.
I lift you my hands and I pray to you ;
I name you my saint for this whole year through.
Oh, bring me my bride, for that were best ;
This were my heaven, and that were my rest.

II.

Saint Joseph! My horse! To my forests of fir!
My senses run mad at the mention of her. . . .
You had better be careless. What comes of it

That you do take care? . . . Nay, call for your
    steed,
Heigh boot and heigh horse, and away with a
    will;
Clutch the rein, seize your horse in his hair and
    speed
Where the hounds call bugle calls over the hill;
And behold! I will follow, for it is not fit
That a man sit singing sad rhymes all day
As a love-sick swain or a maiden may.

A STORM IN VENICE.

I.

THE pent sea throbbed as if wracked with
    pain.
Some black clouds rose and suddenly rode
Right into the town.   The thunder strode
As a giant striding from star to star,
Then turned upon earth and frantically came,
Shaking the hollow heaven.   And far
And near red lightning in ribbon and skein
Did write upon heaven Jehovah's name.

II.

Then lightnings went weaving like shuttle-cocks,
Weaving black raiment of clouds for death;
The mute doves flew to Saint Mark in flocks,
And men stood leaning with gathered breath.
Black gondolas flew as never before,
And drew like crocodiles up on the shore;

And vessels at sea stood further at sea,
And seamen hauled with a bended knee.
Then canvas came down to left and to right;
And ships stood stripped as if stripped for fight!

A HAIL STORM IN VENICE.

I.

THE hail like cannon-shot struck the sea
  And churned it white as a creamy foam;
Then hail like battle-shot struck where we
Stood looking a-sea from a sea-girt home —
Came shooting askance as if shot at the head;
Then glass flew shivered and men fell down
And prayed where they fell, and half the town
Lay riddled and helpless as if shot dead.

II.

Then lightning right full in the eyes! and then
Fair women fell down right flat on the face,
And prayed their pitiful Mother with tears,
And prayed black death as a hiding-place;

And good priests prayed for the sea-bound men
As never good priests had prayed for years. . . .
Then God spake thunder!   And then the rain!
The great, white, beautiful, high-born rain!

FAREWELL TO THE LION OF SAINT MARK.

I.

THERE are sobs of the sea, there is blown
   black rain.
Lo! under the lion and alone in the dark,
Shall I stand as I stand by this sea again?
Yet trait'rous old lion that lords Saint Mark,
I curse you and hate you as ever I can ;
I curse you and hate you my whole heart thro',
Your bible, your book with its Rights of Man :
For I named you my saint, and I prayed to you,
And where is my love, and who has been true?

II.

O vain old lion of lonesome Saint Mark,
With cornice in fashion of blown sea-foam,
High-lifted and light as white clouds in the
   dark, —
When is the rest, and oh where is my home?

Thy brass steeds plunge through the dark in stud,
There are seas to the left and seas to the right,
Front and aback there is nothing but flood,
Nothing but billows and nothing but night.

III.

City at sea, thou art surely an ark,
Sea-blown and a-wreck in the rain and dark.
Lo! white sea-caps that are toss'd and curled.
Thy sins they were many — and behold the
 flood!
And here and about us are the beasts in stud,
Creatures and beasts that creep and go,
Enough, ay, and wicked enough I know,
To populate or devour a world.

IV.

O wrinkled old lion, looking down
With brazen frown upon mine and me,
From tower a-top of your watery town,
Old king of the desert, made king of the sea:
Lo! here is a lesson for thee to-day,
Proud and immovable monarch, I say,
Lo! here is a lesson to-day for thee
Of the things that were and the things to be.

V.

Dank palaces held by the populous sea
For the good dead men, all covered with shell, —
We will pay them a visit some day ; and we,
We may come to love their old palaces well.
Bah ! toppled old columns that tumble across,
Toss'd in the waters that lift and fall,
Waving in waves long masses of moss,
Toppled old columns, — and that will be all.

VI.

Yea, surly old beast with a wrinkled brow,
Sullen old sea-king courting the tide,
Proud old monarch set high in the sea, —
This is the lesson it leaves for thee :
Nothing has been that abideth now,
Nothing is now but will not be,
Nothing shall be that shall abide.

VENICE, 1874.

AFTER ALL.

I.

BY the populous land, on the lonesome sea,
    Lo! these were the gifts of the gods to
      men, —
Three miserable gifts, and only three:
    To love, to forget, to die — and then?

II.

To love in peril and in bitter-sweet pain,
    And then, forgotten, lie down and die:
One moment of sun, whole seasons of rain,
    Then night is rolled to the door of the sky.

III.

To love?   To sit at her feet and to weep;
    To climb to her face, hide your face in her hair;
To nestle you there like a babe in its sleep,
    And, too, like a babe, to believe — it stings
      there!

IV.

To love ? 'Tis to suffer. " Lie close to my breast,
  Like a fair ship in haven, O darling," I cried.
" Your round arms outreaching to heaven for rest
  Make signal to death." . . . Death came, and
    love died.

V.

To forget? To forget, mount horse and clutch
    sword,
  Take ship and make sail to the ice-prison'd seas.
Write books and preach lies; range lands; or
    go hoard
  A grave full of gold, and buy wines — and
    drink lees:

VI.

Then die; and die cursing, and call it a prayer!
  Is earth but a top — a boy-god's delight,
To be spun for his pleasure, while man's despair
  Breaks out like a wail of the damned through
    the night?

VII.

Sit down in the darkness and weep with me
  On the edge of the world. Lo, love lies dead!
And the earth and the sky, and the sky and the
    sea,
  Seem shutting together as a book that is read.

VIII.

Yet what have we learned? We laughed with
    delight
  In the morning at school, and kept toying with
    all
Time's silly playthings. Now, wearied ere night,
  We must cry for dark-mother, her cradle the
    pall.

Rome, 1874.

MAIME MIA.

THE quest of love?   'Tis the quest of
    troubles ;
'Tis the wind through the woods of the Oregon.
Sit down, sit down, for the world goes on
Precisely the same ; and the rainbow bubbles
Of love, they gather, or break, or blow,
Whether you bother your brain or no ;
And for all your troubles, and all your tears,
'Twere'just the same in a hundred years.

Rome, 1874.

THE WINGED LION ONCE MORE.

THE Venetians will tell you that this wonderful work of art was fashioned in Babylon by the sons of Nimrod. Also, that before it was taken from Venice by Napoleon the Great its eyes were made of diamonds, so large and luminous that they lighted up all that part of the city.

Mr. Ruskin says there is no authority for giving this wonderful creation such great antiquity. He is inclined to call it the work of the thirteenth century; but equally without authority, as he admits. To me it is the most simple and sublime thing in the world. Seen in the night, high over the sea and the circle of gaslights, the broken clouds blowing over the large low moon — it is worth a journey round the world to behold it!

I must admit that, in the many verses to my grand old idol, I have been careless of facts. In truth, I know little about the history of the Lion of St. Mark save what the Venetians told me. I never owned a guide-book; and I never in all my travels read a book on Art. In fact, I met so many fools who had read books on Art, that I was afraid to try the experiment.

Napoleon had the lion taken down from the column where it had stood for nearly five hundred years; and in the open book, on which the foot is planted, he caused to be written "The Rights of Man."

When the lion was restored, the Venetians said, "It is indeed our dear old lion, only he has turned over a new leaf!"

I.

WINGED old beast of the burning sands,
    Captive and rover of north-south lands:
Say, what saw you in the land of the Gaul?
In the days when they clutched at thy mane,
    and when
They wrote in thy bible the Rights of Men?
Wrote them and read them,— and that was all.

II.

What saw you in that land, I say,
That land of change, and of gifted mad men?
Silent old lion, say, what have you seen?
Nothing but gleaming of steel, I ween,
Nothing but marching of men, as when
Men shall march in the Judgment Day.

III.

This' is the story the whole world through.
Austrian or Frank, or king or queen,
In the name of freedom to plunder you:
Nay, nothing but this has any man seen
In your watery world where might has been
    right,
Since God first reached from the dark the light.

9

IV.

Rumbling of cannon and neighing of steed —
The worship of strength. Lo! Tuscan and Gaul,
They were gods in their turn. Glory and greed
Did set and unsettle thy whole world's creed;
And thy Christ, O lion, did rise and fall
By the feats of strength. Take heed, take heed,
Lest thy God shall depend on a cannon ball!

VENICE, 1874.

CAVALIER vs. CAVALIER.

I.

NO, no whit jealous of him was I:
  I had sat at his table, tasted his wine,
Broken his bread, as he had mine —
And I would to heaven I had broken his head!
I had shot at him once, and let him try
His hand meantime ten paces at me.
He missed his mark, while I you see,
At the last year's carnival down at Rome,
Troubled his seconds to carry him home.

II.

Well, it fell out thus in a revelry:
We had sat at his table the whole night through,
There were vessels of gold, great cups, mark you,
That were sacred indeed unto better things
Than midnight orgies and revellings;
Then at morn he said, as he toss'd his wine,

Tauntingly, too, of this love of mine,
" A woman to win! the way is free!
I have my gold, you have your wit —
Time will tell us what comes of it!"

A PRINCE OF ROME.

I.

AY, dashing is he indeed, and bold
    As any young Cæsar, and handsome too.
And when he enters the proudest hall,
He doffs his hat, for he stands so tall. . . .
But where do you reckon he got his gold?
Now it might have been from that galleon
That sank, as we know, an age ago
Off the gray coast of Mexico.

II.

But listen to me. One morn last year,
When he did not limp for that taunt and sneer
At my one fair love, — we were strangers then,
And I knew him only as a prince of men, —
Why, we two rode the Campagna plain
That stretches away to the west of Rome,
When sudden he turned to St. Peter's dome,
And, stretching his hand toward the Vatican,
He laughed like a giant, he cursed like a man:
Cried, "Gold!" then sank to his saddle again.

III.

A curious old Spanish proverb says
That many and various are the bits of leather
Saint Crispin uses to make one boot;
And that never was boot without its foot,
To fit it as neat as a glove, and suit
The one to the other in all the ways.
Well, then, put this and put that together,
Fragments of fact like fragments of leather,
And know in the end what you may know
Of that same prince Pimos from Mexico.

IV.

Well, this is the story that a brown monk tells,
A gray-bearded Capucin monk of Rome,
Who hobbles about in the bleak bone cells,
In that strange old nest of the Capucin;
For much he has journey'd and much he has seen:
One time, on the borders of Mexico,
A grizzled old seaman came bent and slow,
And leading a boy, and imploring a home,
Outholding two handsfull of gold for it;
Two great hands shaking like an ague fit.

V.

They smiled at his gold, as the good monks do,
But gave him a home, with all their heart;
And no one questioned and no one cared
What his history, place, or part—
Only to know that the wayfarer shared
Their home content. The bright boy grew
Into man's estate, but wild as the wind;
And, leaving the convent walls behind,
Oft he would wander the whole year through:
But why he wandered away, or where,
There was none to question, and but one to care.

VI.

Well, there be men who are ready to swear
That they saw this same prince years ago,
With his princely air and his princely ease,
Astride of his mule, with his saddle-bow
Swung with pistols, as he rode on down
The mountain trail to the mountain town:
His long hair blown in the mountain breeze,
And a brigand's badge of command high blown
From his feathered hat as he rode alone.

VII.

Then long he ranged in his journeys and far
Over mountains that climbed to the morning
    star.
And the old man died ; but the boy was away, —
Robbing ? — or trading ?   It is much the same :
The same result with a different name.
The shopman he robs you from day to day,
Little by little, that you may not reck ;
Robs you by lies, risks body and soul :
The dashing bold robber he takes the whole,
Tells you the truth, and but risks his neck.

VIII.

. . . And mark ! as he rode with the king last year
Through a marsh of the Tiber, a buffalo,
Humped-backed and horrible, plunged at his
    steed,
When the king struck spurs, and fled in fear.
But he, whipping his lasso as quick as thought,
Threw it, and throttled the beast on the spot.
And who, my prince, I should like to know,
But a vulgar vaquero could do such a deed ?

IX.

But, where did he get his gold? this prince, —
The bright gold eagle and the old doubloon,
The old gold plate, and the great gold spoon,
And the tall gold goblet, and the quaint gold cup
That star his table when he comes to sup?
The gold alone is the question, since
Here, in Italy, princes are — well,
Princes are thicker than fiddlers in hell.

Rome, 1873.

GAMBLER OR PRINCE?

I.

NOW some have said, and so may you,
 It was nobody's business, while the man
  could hold
His head like a prince and bear him true,
Where the gambler picked up his gold,
Or whether the prince was à prince or not.
And then, when it cost you a pistol shot
To ask the question, 'twas overbold
To question at all. But then my friend
Would know who he was; and he fought to this
 end.

II.

One night, as he sat with his goblets of gold,
He mentioned the name of my brave friend's sire;
And very complacently sat and told
That he himself was this great man's son.
Vengeance and fury! My friend was on fire!
The man sprang up as if shot from a gun,

And he thrust the lie in his teeth ; and then
Asked where was his family founded, and when?
He then sat down, and a pistol shot
Was all the answer that any one got.
They fought at dawn : shot square thro' the head,
The gypsy-stol'n brother and prince lay dead.

NAPLES, 1874.

A PEASANT'S PLEA.

I.

HAD he made her his spouse like a man, why
    then,
Still might he doff his tall plume to men;
Had he loved like a prince, had she loved him
    true,
Why, I could have waited her life-time through;
Could have crossed and have waited on the other
    side,
With my two hands held to my coming bride:
For the days of the earth they be but a day
That lie like a shadow across life's way,
And a brief night-land that divides the sea
Of the years that were from the years to be.

II.

But to know that she lay in his arms in sin,
That the great strong beast arose from the feast
And went to my bride he had bought with his
    gold! . . .

Ha! the night after that — why, they called in a
    priest
To pray for a prince who was found all cold
In a narrow canal, with his head crushed in —
Perhaps by a tile! . . . Oh, the blessed sweet
    pain
Of revenge, as I fled to my mountains again!

MILAN, 1873.

A DREAM OF VENICE.

I.

THERE are doves overhead, going in, blow-
　　ing out;
They are wooing and cooing and talking of love,
The white and the gray and the purple-robed
　　dove.
They are billing and cooing and flying about
By the high chiselled capital, cornice, and that:
And I envy them, hate them, I curse thereat,
And I call " Oh, my love!"　Cold echoes come
　　back
As if hurled from the walls and sent hounding
　　my track.

II.

Now let us turn back from the watery town;
Let the water-rat build; let the cornice above
Change color from clouds of the purple-necked
　　dove;
Let the yellow-sailed sea-craft ride pleasantly
　　down.

Let the soft morning sun lie in long broken
    bars
'Gainst the tall palace walls. Let us go from
    the land
Of the bride of my soul with the small dimpled
    hand,
That I led through the outermost reach of red
    stars.

FOR THE NILE.

I.

WHAT! turn me from Venice? To leave
  her at last!
This city I loved in my search through the vast
And the unnamed seas of the universe?
To turn me for aye from this face of hers?
St. Joseph! To dream it could come to this!
You never have known, then, what love is!

II.

I am lone as Marius 'mid ruins could be.
Yea, a sea of fair people that walk by the sea
In the cool of the morn by St. Mark; and they
  talk
Of the things that are nearest the heart as they
  walk,
And all are made glad. But, Christ! as for me!

III.

Lo! I shall depart and I know not where;
Let the men be brave, let the maids be fair,
Let the wrinkled old lion that tops the town
Now ruffle his mane, St. Theodore frown, —
It is nothing to me. I shall love but the one,
This one fair city that is under the sun.

IV.

I shall bear her afar and anywhere;
I have hid my heart in the gold of her hair. . . .
Her fair holy face, her great soft eyes,
Liquid with love. Her soul's surprise,
Then the calm delight that the world is aware
When she rests in ruins, like the curtains of
    skies.

VENICE, 1874.

VESPERS IN SAN MARCO.

THE four brazen horses! unbridled as when
    This Venice was Venice, and the wise
    led the brave
Through the gates of the Turk, through the
    turbulent main,
And led the steeds home from the Hellespont, —
They plunge in the gaslight as bridled again.
The vast ducal palace frowns dark in the wave,
The white Bridge of Sighs — a brief, narrow
    span —
Draws back in a chasm. The grand gilded
    dome,
Where the doves of St. Mark all the year have
    their home,
Sounds hollow and deep like a far plashing
    font.

RECOLLECTION.

I.

WE dwelt in the woods of the Tippecanoe,
   In a lone lost cabin with never the view
Of the full day's sun for the whole year thro' . . .
With strange half-hints through the russet corn
We children were hurried one night. Next
   morn
There was frost in the trees, and a sprinkle of
   snow,
And tracks on the ground. Three boys below
The low eaves listened. We opened the door,
And a girl baby cried, — and then we were four.

II.

We were not sturdy, and we were not wise
In the things of the world or the ways of men.
A pale-browed mother with a prophet's eyes,
A father that dreamed and looked anywhere. .

Three brothers, — wild blossoms, tall-fashioned
    and fair ;
And we mingled with none, but we lived as
    when
The pair first lived ere they knew the fall ;
And, loving all things, we believed in all.

III.

Ah ! girding yourself and throwing your strength
On the front of a forest that stands in mail
Sounds gallant, indeed, in a pioneer's tale.
But, God in heaven ! the weariness
Of a sweet soul banished to a life like this !
This reaching of weary-worn arms full length ;
This stooping all day to the stubborn cold soil —
This holding the heart ! it is more than toil !
What loneness of heart ! What wishings to die
In that soul in the earth, that was born for the
    sky !

IV.

We parted wood-curtains, pushed westward, and
    we,
Why, we wandered and wandered a half year
    through ;

We tented with herds as the Arabs do,
And at last sat down by the sundown sea.
Then there in that sun did my soul take fire!
It burned in its fervor, thou Venice, for thee!
My glad heart glowed with the one desire
To stride to the front, to live, to be!
To strow great thoughts through the world as
 I went,
As God sows stars through the firmament.

 Venice, 1874.

TORCELLO.

THE sometime song of gondolier
    Is heard afar.   The fishermen
Betimes draw net by ruined shore,
In full spring-time when east winds fall;
Then traders row with muffled oar,
Then long-leg birds stretch neck, and then —
Tedesca or the turban'd Turk,
The pirate, at some midnight work
By watery wall, — but that is all.

Note. — The author begs to apologize for reprinting from
an earlier volume this and the two following pieces, which
appropriately belong to "Songs of Italy."

ATTILA'S THRONE: TORCELLO.

I.

I DO recall some sad days spent
  By borders of the Orient,
Days sweet as sad to memory . . .
'Twould make a tale.   It matters not . . .
I sought the loneliest seas ; I sought
The solitude of ruins, and forgot
Mine own lone life and littleness
Before this fair land's mute distress,
That sat within this changeful sea.

II.

Slow sailing through the reedy isles,
By unknown banks, through unknown bays,
Some sunny, summer yesterdays,
Where Nature's beauty still beguiles,
I watched the storied yellow sail
And lifted prow of steely mail.
'Tis all that's left Torcello now, —
A pirate's yellow sail, a prow.

III.

Below the far, faint peaks of snow,
And grass-grown causeways well below,
I touched Torcello.

              Once on land,
I took a sea-shell in my hand,
And blew like any trumpeter.
I felt the fig-leaves lift and stir
On trees that reach from ruined wall
Above my head, — but that was all.
Back from the farther island shore
Came echoes trooping — nothing more.

IV.

Yet here stood Adria once, and here
Came Attila with sword and flame,
And set his throne of hollowed stone
In her high mart.

           And it remains
Still lord o'er all.   Where once the tears
Of mute petition fell, the rains
Of heaven fall.   Lo! all alone
There lifts this massive empty throne!
The sea has changed his meed, his mood,
And made this sedgy solitude.

V.

By cattle paths grass-grown and worn,
Through marbled streets all stain'd and torn
By time and battle, lone I walked.
A bent old beggar, white as one
For better fruitage blossoming,
Came on.   And as he came he talked
Unto himself; for there are none
In all his island, old and dim,
To answer back or question him.

VI.

I turned, retraced my steps once more.
The hot miasma steamed and rose
In deadly vapor from the reeds
That grew from out the shallow shore,
Where peasants say the sea-horse feeds,
And Nepture shapes his horn and blows

VII.

I climb'd and sat that throne of stone
To contemplate, to dream, to reign —
Ay, reign above myself; to call
The people of the past again

Before me as I sat alone
In all my kingdom.

There were kine
That browsed along the reedy brine,
And now and then a tusky boar
Would shake the high reeds of the shore,
A bird blow by, — but that was all.

VIII.

I watched the lonesome sea-gull pass.
I did remember and forget, —
The past rolled by; I stood alone.
I sat the shapely chiselled stone
That stands in tall sweet grasses set;
Ay, girdle deep in long strong grass,
And green alfalfa.

Very fair
The heavens were, and still and blue,
For Nature knows no changes there.
The Alps of Venice, far away,
Like some half-risen large moon lay.

IX.

How sweet the grasses at my feet!·
The smell of clover over sweet.
· I heard the hum of bees.   The bloom
Of clover-tops and cherry-trees
Were being rifled by the bees,
And these were building in a tomb.

X.

The fair alfalfa — such as has
Usurped the Occident, and grows
With all the sweetness of the rose
On Sacramento's sundown hills —
Is there, and that dead island fills
With fragrance.   Yet the smell of death
Comes riding in on every breath.

XI.

Lo! death that is not death, but rest:
To step aside, to watch and wait
Beside the wave, outside the gate,
With all life's pulses in your breast:
To absolutely rest, to pray
In some lone mountain while you may.

XII.

That sad sweet fragrance.　It had sense,
And sound, and voice.　It was a part
Of that which had possessed my heart,
And would not of my will go hence.
'Twas Autumn's breath ; 'twas dear as kiss
Of any worshipped woman is.

XIII.

Some snails had climb'd the throne and writ
Their silver monograms on it
In unknown tongues.
　　　　　　　　I sat thereon,
I dreamed until the day was gone ;
I blew again my pearly shell, —
Blew long and strong, and loud and well ;
I puffed my cheeks, I blew, as when
Horn'd satyrs danced the delight of men.

XIV.

Some mouse-brown cows that fed within
Looked up.　A cowherd rose hard by,
My single subject, clad in skin,
Nor yet half-clad.

I caught his eye, —
He stared at me, then turned and fled.
He frightened fled, and as he ran,
Like wild beast from the face of man,
Across his shoulder threw his head.

XV.

He gathered up his skin of goat
About his breast and hairy throat;
He stopped, and then this subject true,
Mine only one in all the isle,
Turned round, and, with a fawning smile,
Came back and asked me for a *sou!*

SANTA MARIA: TORCELLO.

I.

AND yet again through the watery miles
    Of reeds I rowed, till the desolate isles
Of the black bead-makers of Venice were not.
I touched where a single sharp tower is shot
To heaven, and torn by thunder and rent ·
As if it had been Time's battlement.
A city lies dead, and this great gravestone
Stands on its grave like a ghost alone.

II.

Some cherry-trees grow here, and here
An old church, simple and severe
In ancient aspect, stands alone
Amid the ruin and decay, all grown
In moss and grasses.
             Old and quaint,
With antique cuts of martyr'd saint,
The gray church stands with stooping knees,
Defying the decay of seas.

III.

Her pictured Hell, with flames blown high,
In bright mosaics wrought and set
When man first knew the Nubian art,
Her bearded saints as black as jet,
Her quaint Madonna, dim with rain
And touch of pious lips of pain,
So touched my lonesome soul, that I
Gazed long, then came and gazed again,
And loved, and took her to my heart.

IV.

Nor monk in black, nor Capucin,
Nor priest of any creed was seen.
A sun-browned woman, old and tall,   .
And still as any shadow is,
Stole forth from out the mossy wall
With massive keys to show me this:
Came slowly forth, and, following,
Three birds — and all with drooping wing.

V.

Three mute brown babes of hers; and they —
Oh, they were beautiful as sleep,

Or death, below the troubled deep!
And on the pouting lips of these,
Red corals of the silent seas,
Sweet birds, the everlasting seal
Of silence that the God has set
On this dead island sits for aye.

VI.

I would forget, yet not forget
Their helpless eloquence. They creep
Somehow into my heart, and keep
One bleak, cold corner, jewel set.
They steal my better self away
To them, as little birds that day
Stole fruits from out the cherry-trees.

VII.

So helpless and so wholly still,
So sad, so wrapt in mute surprise,
That I did love, despite my will.
One little maid of ten — such eyes,
So large and lonely, so divine!
Such pouting lips, such pearly cheek! —

Did lift her perfect eyes to mine,
Until our souls did touch and speak —
Stood by me all that perfect day,
Yet not one sweet word could she say.

VIII.

She turned her melancholy eyes
So constant to my own, that I .
Forgot the going clouds, the sky ;
Found fellowship, took bread and wine :
And so her little soul and mine
Stood very near together there.
And oh, I found her very fair !
Yet not one soft word could she say :
What did she think of all that day ?

LILIAN.

I.

SHE is dark as Israel.   She is proud and still
  As Lebanon pine on the Palatine Hill.
Her name it is Lilla ; a plain, pretty name
That syllables by quite simple and tame,
Until you have looked on her presence ; and
    then ! —
Oh, it then means to you, as to me it has meant,
The fairest thing under the firmament.

II.

Her name is as language ; and, when I know
Nor name nor type to give utterance to
My grandest conception of woman, she
Stands up in my soul, calm, silently,
And fills the blank with her own sweet name.
Ay, even at mention of her I grow —
Grow grand and splendid as is growing flame.

III.

Thou dark silent pine of the Palatine Hill!
Thou princess and empress, I look to thee still,
Disdain as you will; for my gods they must be.
Yea, regal my soul, and, having known thee,
How can I to others bow knee or bend will?...
Now, come what comes, my whole life through
I shall be the nobler for this love of you.

LIFE.

L IFE ? 'Tis the story of love and of troubles,
     Of troubles and love, that travel together
The round world through.   Behold the bubbles
Of love ! Then troubles and turbulent weather.
Why, man had all Eden ! Then love, then Cain !
Go away, go away with your bitter-sweet pain
Of love, and leave us!   Come ! care not a pin,
Until peace goes out, and till love comes in.

NAPLES, 1874.

IN PÈRE LA CHAISE.

I.

A N avenue of tombs! I stand before
  The tomb of Abelard and Eloise.
A long, a dark bent line of cypress trees
Leads past and on to other shrines ; but o'er
This tomb the boughs hang darkest and most
    dense,
Like leaning mourners clad in black. The sense
Of awe oppresses you. This solitude
Means more than common sorrow. Down the
    wood
Still lovers pass, then pause, then turn again,
And weep like silent, unobtrusive rain.

II.

'Tis but a simple, antique tomb that kneels
As one that weeps above the broken clay.
'Tis stained with storms, 'tis eaten well away,
Nor half the old-new story now reveals

Of heart that held beyond the tomb to heart.
But oh, it tells of love!   And that true page
Is more in this cold, hard, commercial age,
When love is calmly counted some lost art,
Than all man's mighty monuments of war
Or archives vast of art and science are.

III.

Here poets pause and dream a listless hour;
Here silly pilgrims stoop and kiss the clay;
Here sweetest maidens leave a cross or flower,
While vandals bear the tomb in bits away.
The ancient stone is scarred with name and
   scrawl
Of many tender fools.   But over all,
And high above all other scrawls, is writ
One simple thing, most touching and most fit.
Some pitying soul has tiptoed high above,
And with a nail has scrawled but this: "O
   Love!"

IV.

O Love! . . . I turn; I climb the hill of tombs,
Where sleeps the "bravest of the brave," below,
His bed of scarlet blooms in zone of snow —
No cross nor sign, save this red bed of blooms.

I see grand tombs to France's lesser dead, —
Colossal steeds, white pyramids, still red
At base with blood, still torn with shot and shell,
To testify that here the Commune fell:
And yet I turn once more from all of these,
And stand before the tomb of Eloise.

PARIS, 1872.

LONGING FOR HOME.

I.

COULD I but return to my woods once more,
  And dwell in their depths as I have dwelt,
Kneel in their mosses as I have knelt,
Sit where the cool white rivers run,
Away from the world and half hid from the sun,
Hear wind in the woods of my storm-torn shore,
Glad to the heart with listening, —
It seems to me that I then could sing,
And sing as I never have sung before.

II.

I miss, how wholly I miss my wood,
My matchless, magnificent dark-leaved firs
That climb up the terrible heights of Hood,
Where only the breath of white heaven stirs!
These Alps they are barren; wrapped in storms,
Formless masses of Titan forms,
They loom like ruins of a grandeur gone,
And lonesome as death to look upon.

III.

O God! once more in my life to hear
The voice of a wood that is loud and alive,
That stirs with its being like a vast bee-hive!
And oh, once more in my life to see
The great bright eyes of the antlered deer;
To sing with the birds that sing for me,
To tread where only the red man trod,
To say no word, but listen to God!

VERONA, 1873.

PESTAM.

THIS land it is desolate, dead as death!
 Never the sound of a beast or a bird,
Nor voices of Nature above a breath;
Never the wild deer's quick retreat,
Never the pheasant's far drum-beat:
Only the hideous marsh buffalo,
With a half-choked moan or a lazy low;
Only the dull cloven tramp of the herd;
Only the tiresome gray outlook;
Only the tourist tight holding a book,
A red-bound book as a lamp for his feet!

PESTAM, 1873.

TITIAN'S LAND.

I.

I JOURNEYED to Titian's torn land last year,
To make me companions of peaks as of old:
The gray peaks lifted their granite brows
As barren and cold as a virgin's vows.
I saw and was silent. Unutterable thought
Was mine, and a boyhood's memory rolled
On past; and I gave to the past a tear.
I lived dead days that were best forgot.

II.

I listened for bird, for beast. Lo! a gloom
Had mantled the land like a mournful cloud,
And lay like the solitude guarding a tomb.
I spake and made sign — but they answered me
    not.
I lifted my hands and I called aloud —
Then echoes went rolling from cliff to cloud,
And peasants came cautious, strange-clad and
    tall:
Echoes and peasants, — and that was all:

III.

Wild peasants that cling to the cliffs, and reap,
With short broad scythes, the adventurous grain;
Then peasants that dwell by the timbered steep,
In mossy caverns or in leafy low tents,
And fall the tall forest and plant again
The orderly woods like to regiments ;
And fashion the beam and hew the wood,
And guide the raft through the foamy flood.

Como, 1874.

IN INNSBRUCK.

DAY by day by the high-born rills
  That plunge into Innsbruck born of the
    snow,
I list for the voices of long ago.
I stood over Ishl hid under the hills;
I stood where the white clouds curled and broke
In the morn, like puffs of battle-white smoke:
I listened all day, but listened in vain,
For the voice of my mountain comes never again.

INNSBRUCK.

FOR PRINCESS MAUD.

I.

STORM in the east and storm in the west,
　　And the wild sea over my head;
But oh, the storm that is in my breast
For my brave love three days dead!
Storm and tempest, and peril and pain,
Nothing but tempest and wild white rain.

II.

Dead is my heart in the dust to-day,
And the wheels go over my head.
Will never the stone be rolled away
From the grave of my beautiful dead?
Storm in my heart, on the hill, on the plain;
Tempest and tears, and the wild white rain.

III.

Under the storm and the cloud to-day,
And to-day the hard peril and pain —
To-morrow the stone shall be rolled away,
For the sunshine shall follow the rain.
Merciful Father, I will not complain,
I know that the sunshine shall follow the rain.

I SHALL REMEMBER.

I.

DID I court fame by the favor of man?
    Make war upon creed, or strike hand with
    clan?
I sang my songs of the sounding trees,
As careless of name or of fame as the sea;
And these I sang for the love of these,
And the sad sweet solace they brought to me.
I but sang for myself, touched here, touched there,
Like a strong-winged bird that flies anywhere.

II.

Did I the religions assail?   Gainsay
One creed that is taught, or lift hard hand,
Or teach aught else than as Christ taught? Nay,
There is little enough of love in the land,
There is little enough of Faith for me,
There is little enough of Charity,

Little enough of Hope, I guess, —
And I am the last to make these less.
And yet did ye stone your prophets ; and yet —
Well, I shall remember, though ye may forget.

VENICE, 1873.

12

VALE.

I.

LET us say farewell.   A far dim spark
    Illumes my path.   The light of my day
Hath fled, and yet I am far away.
The small curled moon has dipped her horn
In the dark'ning sea.   High up, in the dark
The wrinkled old lion, he looks away
To the east, and impatient as if for morn. . . .
I have gone the girdle of earth, and say,
What have I gained but a temple gray,
Two crow's-feet, and a heart forlorn.

II.

A star starts yonder like a soul afraid !
It falls like a thought thro' the great profound.
Fearfully swift and with never a sound,
It fades into nothing, as all things fade.

Yea, what is the world? And where is the leaven
In the pride of name or a proud man's nod?
Oh tiresome, tiresome stairs to heaven!
Weary, oh wearisome ways to God!
'Twere better to sit with the chin on the palm,
Slow tapping the sand, come storm, come calm.

III.

I have lived from within and not from without;
I have drunk from a fount, have fed from a hand
That no man knows who lives upon land;
I care not a pin for the praise of men:
And yet my soul it is crying out
In hunger for love. I starve, I die,
Each day of my life. Ye pass me by
Each day, and laugh as ye pass; and when
Ye come, I start in my place as ye come,
And lean, and would speak, — but my lips are
    dumb.

IV.

Those sliding stars and the changeful moon!
Let me rest on the plains of Lombardy for aye,
Or sit down by the Adrian Sea and die.
The days that do seem as an afternoon,

They all are here.   I am strong and true
To myself; can pluck and can plant anew
My heart, and grow tall ; could come to be
Another being ; lift bolder hand
And conquer.   Yet ever will come to me
The thought that Italia is not my land.

V.

A time you may sit and be satisfied ;
You may toy with new things like a child at play ;
But you rise at last and you thrust them away :
And then there rises a Saxon's pride,
And the heart fills full, and it throbs to burst,
With a sense of wrong, and a savage sense
Of right ; and you rise and you look afar,
And over the seas where the spaces are,
And you feel that there the God at the first
Did set you down with inheritance.

VI.

Here too are the mountains.   But a day from
        this town
Of marble, that sits to its waist in the sea,
A moon-white mountain of snow looks down
On a thousand glories of old Italy.

And the seas are here, and the sunlit skies
Look soft as a love in a lover's eyes, —
Yet all this beauty and love by the sea
But seems to mock me, and but seems to say,
" Stranger, lorn stranger, rise ! go your way ! "

VII.

I shall find diversion with another kind,
There are roads on the land and roads on the sea,
Take ship and sail, and sail till I find
The love that I sought from eternity.
Run away from oneself, take ship and sail
The middle white seas, see turbaned men, —
Throw thought to the dogs for aye. And when
All seas are travelled and all scenes shall fail,
Why, then this doubtful, sad gift of verse
Will save me from death — or something worse.

VIII.

Then deep-tangled woodland and wild waterfall,
Oh farewell for aye, till the judgment day !
I shall see you no more, O land of mine,
O half-aware land like a child at play !
O voiceless and vast as the pushed-backed skies !

No more, blue seas in the blest sunshine,
No more, black woods where the white peaks rise,
No more, bleak plains where the high winds fall,
Or the red man cries or the shrill birds call!

IX.

My hand it is weary, and my harp unstrung;
And where is the good that I pipe or sing,
Fashion new notes, or shape any thing?
The songs of my rivers remain unsung
Henceforward for me. . . . But a man shall rise
From the great vast valleys of the Occident, ·
With hand on his harp of gold, and with eyes
That lift with glory and a proud intent;
Yet so gentle indeed, that his sad heart-strings
Shall thrill to your heart of hearts as he sings.

X.

Let the wind sing songs in the lakeside reeds,
Lo, I shall be less than the indolent wind!
Why should I sow, when I reap and bind
And gather in nothing but the pasture weeds?
It is best I abide let what will befall,

To rest if I can, let time roll by ;
Let others endeavor to learn, while I,
With nought to conceal, with much to regret,
Shall sit and endeavor, alone, to forget.

XI.

Shall I shape pipes from these seaside reeds,
And play for the children, and shout and call ?
Lo ! men they have mocked me the whole year
    through !
Nay, let us not laugh.   I find in old creeds,
And in quaint old tongues, a world that is new ;
And these, I will gather the sweets of them all.
And the old-time doctrines and the old-time signs,
I will taste of them all, as tasting old wines.

XII.

I will find new thought, as a new-found vein
Of rock-locked gold in my far, fair West.
I will rest and forget, will entreat to be blest ;
Take up new thought and again grow young ;
Yea, take a new world as one born again,
And never hear more mine own mother tongue ;
Nor miss it.   Why should I?   I never once heard,
In my land's language, love's one sweet word.

XIII.

. . . . How I do wander!   And yet why not?
I once had a song, told a tale in rhyme;
Wrote books indeed in my proud young prime:
I aimed at the heart like a musket ball,
I struck curs'd folly like a cannon shot, —
And where is the glory or good of it all?
Yet these did I write for my love, but this
I write for myself, — and it is as it is.

XIV.

Yea, storms have blown counter and shaken me.
And yet was I fashioned for strife, and strong
And daring of heart, and born to endure:
My soul sprang upward, my feet felt sure;
My faith was as wide as a wide-boughed tree.
But there be limits; and a sense of wrong
For ever before you will make you less
A man, than a man at the first would guess.

XV.

Good men can forgive — and, they say, forget. . . .
Far less of the angel than Indian is set
In my stern soul.   And I look away
To a land that is dearer than this, and say,

" I shall remember, though you may forget.
Yea, I shall remember for aye and a day
The keen taunts thrown in a boy face, when
He cried unto God for the love of men."

XVI.

Enough, ay and more than enough, of this!
I know that the sunshine must follow the rain;
And if this be the winter, why, spring again
Will come in its season, full blossomed in bliss.
I will lean to the storm, though the winds blow
    strong;
Yea, the winds they have blown and have shaken
    me —
As the winds blow songs through a shattered
    tree,
They have blown this broken and careless-set
    song.

XVII.

They have sung this song, be it never so bad;
Have blown upon me and played upon me,
Have broken the notes, — blown sad, blown glad;
Just as the winds blow fierce and free

A barren, a blighted, and a curs'd fig tree.
And if I grow careless and heed no whit
Whether it please or what comes of it,
Why, talk to the winds then, and not to me!

VENICE, 1875.

Cambridge: Press of John Wilson & Son.